"Can we just say I'm tired of playing games and leave it at that? I want to be close to you because I like you for yourself. So do you want the same thing or have I misread the signs?"

"No, you haven't," she admitted. "But you said just this afternoon that I was a complication you didn't need."

"Over-analyzing is second nature to me. It's saved my skin more often than I care to count. But in this case I took it too far."

"Maybe not," she said judiciously. "Maybe you simply realized there was no future in a relationship with me."

"Never counting on the future is another by-product of my job. The only certainty is the here and now."

He took a step toward her, then another, until he was close enough to inhale the scent of her skin. "What do you say, Emily?" he asked hoarsely. "Will you take a chance with me?"

Catherine Spencer, once an English teacher, fell into writing through eavesdropping on a conversation about Harlequin® Romances. Within two months she changed careers, and sold her first book to Mills & Boon® in 1984. She moved to Canada from England thirty years ago and lives in Vancouver. She is married to a Canadian and has four grown children—two daughters and two sons (and now eight grandchildren)—plus two dogs. In her spare time she plays the piano, collects antiques, and grows tropical shrubs.

You can visit Catherine Spencer's website at www.catherinespencer.com

Recent titles by the same author:

SICILIAN BILLIONAIRE, BOUGHT BRIDE
THE GIANNAKIS BRIDE
THE ITALIAN BILLIONAIRE'S CHRISTMAS MIRACLE

THE GREEK MILLIONAIRE'S SECRET CHILD

BY
CATHERINE SPENCER

MILLS & BOON
Pure reading pleasure™

First published in Great Britain 2009
Harlequin Mills & Boon Limited,
Eton House, 18-24 Paradise Road, Richmond, Surrey TW9 1SR

© Catherine Spencer Books Limited 2009

ISBN: 978 0 263 87204 0

Set in Times Roman 10½ on 12¾ pt
01-0509-46707

Printed and bound in Spain
by Litografia Rosés, S.A., Barcelona

THE GREEK
MILLIONAIRE'S
SECRET CHILD

CHAPTER ONE

EMILY singled him out immediately, not because his father had described him so well that she couldn't miss him, but because even though he stood well back from everyone else, he dominated the throng waiting to meet passengers newly arrived at Athens's Venizelos Airport. At more than six feet of lean, toned masculinity blessed with the face of a fallen angel, he could hardly help it. One look at him was enough to tell her he was the kind of man other men envied, and women fought over.

As if on cue, his gaze locked with hers. Locked and lingered a small eternity, long enough for her insides to roll over in fascinated trepidation. Every instinct of self-preservation told her he was bad news; that she'd live to rue the day she met him. Then he nodded, as though he knew exactly the effect he'd had on her, and cutting a swath through the crowd, strode forward.

Given her first unobstructed view, she noted how his jeans emphasized his narrow hips and long legs, the way his black leather bomber jacket rode smoothly over his powerful shoulders, and the startling contrast of his throat rising strong and tanned against the open collar of his white shirt. As he drew closer, she saw, too, that his mouth and his jaw, the latter firm and faintly dusted with new beard shadow, betrayed the stubbornness his father had spoken of.

When he reached them, he asked in a voice as sinfully seductive as the rest of him, "So you beat the odds and made it back in one piece. How was the flight?"

"Long," Pavlos replied, sounding every bit as worn and weary as he surely must feel. Not even painkillers and the luxury of first-class air travel had been enough to cushion his discomfort. "Very long. But as you can see, I have my guardian angel at my side." He reached over his shoulder, groped for her hand and squeezed it affectionately. "Emily, my dear, I am pleased to introduce my son, Nikolaos. And this, Niko, is my nurse, Emily Tyler. What I would have done without her, I cannot imagine."

Again, Nikolaos Leonidas's gaze lingered, touring the length of her in insolent appraisal. Behind his chiseled good looks lurked a certain arrogance. He was not a man to be crossed, she thought. "*Yiasu,* Emily Tyler," he said.

Even though her sweater and slacks pretty much covered all of her, she felt naked under that sweeping regard. His eyes were the problem, she thought dizzily. Not brown like his father's, as she'd expected, but a deep green reminiscent of fine jade, they added an arresting final touch to a face already possessed of more than its rightful share of dark beauty.

Swallowing, she managed an answering, "*Yiasu.*"

"You speak a little Greek?"

"A very little," she said. "I just exhausted my entire vocabulary."

"That's what I thought."

The comment might have stung if he hadn't tempered it with a smile that assaulted her with such charm, it was all she could do not to buckle at the knees. For heaven's sake, what was the matter with her? She was twenty-seven, and if not exactly the most sexually experienced woman in the world, hardly in the first flush of innocent youth, either. She knew well enough that appearances counted for little. It was the person inside that mattered, and from everything she'd been told, Niko Leonidas fell sadly short in that respect.

His manner as he turned his attention again to Pavlos did nothing to persuade her otherwise. He made no effort to embrace his father, to reassure him with a touch to the shoulder or hand that the old man could count on his son for whatever support he might need during his convalescence. Instead he commandeered a porter to take care of the loaded luggage cart one of the flight attendants had brought, and with a terse, "Well, since we seem to have exhausted the formalities, let's get out of here," marched toward the exit, leaving Emily to follow with Pavlos.

Only when they arrived at the waiting Mercedes did he betray a hint of compassion. "Don't," he ordered, when she went to help her patient out of the wheelchair and with surprising tenderness, scooped his father into his arms, laid him carefully on the car's roomy back seat and draped a blanket over his legs. "You didn't have to do that," Pavlos snapped, trying unsuccessfully to mask a grimace of pain.

Noticing, Niko said, "Apparently I did. Or would you have preferred I stand idly by and watch you fall on your face?"

"I would prefer to be standing on my own two feet without needing assistance of any kind."

"Then you should have taken better care of yourself when you were away—or else had the good sense to stay home in the first place, instead of deciding you had to see Alaska before you die."

Emily was tempted to kick the man, hard, but made do with a glare. "Accidents happen, Mr. Leonidas."

"Especially to globe-trotting eighty-six-year-old men."

"It was hardly his fault that the cruise ship ran aground, nor was he the only passenger on board who was injured. All things considered, and given his age, your father's done amazingly well. In time, and with adequate follow-up physical therapy, he should make a reasonably good recovery."

"And if he doesn't?"

"Then I guess you're going to have to step up to the plate and start acting like a proper son."

He favored her with a slow blink made all the more disturbing by the sweep of his lashes, which were indecently long and silky. "Nurse and family counselor all rolled into one," he drawled. "How lucky is that?"

"Well, you did ask."

"And you told me." He tipped the porter, left him to return the airport's borrowed wheelchair, then slammed closed the car trunk and opened the front passenger door with a flourish. "Climb in. We can continue this conversation later."

As she might have expected, he drove with flair and expertise. Within half an hour of leaving the airport, they were cruising the leafy green streets of Vouliagmeni, the exclusive Athens suburb overlooking the Saronic Gulf on the east coast of the Attic Peninsula, which Pavlos had described to her so vividly. Soon after, at the end of a quiet road running parallel to the beach, Niko steered the car through a pair of ornate wrought-iron gates, which opened at the touch of a remote control button on the dash.

Emily had gathered Pavlos was a man of considerable wealth, but was hardly prepared for the rather frightening opulence confronting her as the Mercedes wound its way up a long curving driveway, and she caught her first sight of…what? His house? Villa? Mansion?

Set in spacious, exquisitely landscaped grounds and screened from local traffic by a stand of pines, the place defied such mundane description. Stucco walls, blindingly white, rose in elegant proportions to a tiled roof as blue as she'd always imagined the skies to be in Athens, even though, this late September afternoon, an approaching storm left them gray and threatening. Long windows opened to wide terraces shaded by pergolas draped in flowering vines. A huge fountain splashed in a central forecourt, peacocks preened and screeched on the lawns, and from somewhere on the seaward side of the property, a dog barked.

She had little time to marvel, though, because barely had the car come to a stop outside a set of double front doors than they opened, and a man in his late fifties or early sixties appeared with a wheelchair light years removed from the spartan model offered by the airport.

The devoted butler, Georgios, she presumed. Pavlos had spoken of him often and with great fondness. Behind him came a younger man, little more than a boy really, who went about unloading the luggage while

Niko and the butler lifted Pavlos from the car to the chair. By the time they were done, he was gray in the face and the grooves paralleling his mouth carved more deeply than usual.

Even Niko seemed concerned. "What can you do for him?" he muttered, cornering Emily near the front entrance as Georgios whisked his employer away down a wide, marble-floored hall.

"Give him something to manage the pain, and let him rest," she said. "The journey was very hard on him."

"He doesn't look to me as if he was fit to travel in the first place."

"He wasn't. Given his age and the severity of his osteoporosis, he really ought to have remained in the hospital another week, but he insisted on coming home, and when your father makes up his mind, there's no changing it."

"Tell me something I don't already know." Niko scowled and shucked off his jacket. "Shall I send for his doctor?"

"In the morning, yes. He'll need more medication than what I was able to bring with us. But I have enough to see him through tonight." Struggling to preserve a professional front despite the fact that Niko stood close enough for the warmth of his body to reach out and touch hers, she sidled past him and took her travel bag from the pile of luggage accumulating inside the front door. "If you'd show me to his room, I really should attend to him now."

He stepped away and led her to the back of the villa, to a large, sun-filled apartment on the main floor. Consisting of a sitting room and bedroom, both with

French doors that opened onto a low-walled patio, it overlooked the gardens and sea. Still in the wheelchair, stationed next to the window in the sitting room, Pavlos leaned forward, drinking in the view which, even swathed in floating mist as the storm closed in, held him transfixed.

"He had this part of the house converted into his private suite a few years ago when the stairs proved too much for him," Niko said in a low voice.

Glancing through to the bedroom, Emily asked, "And the hospital bed?"

"I had it brought in yesterday. He'll probably give me hell for removing the one he's used to, but this one seemed more practical, at least for now."

"You did the right thing. He'll be more comfortable in it, even if he won't be spending much time there except at night."

"Why not?"

"The more mobile he is, the better his chances of eventually walking again, although…"

Picking up on the reservation in her voice, Niko pounced on it. "Although what? You said earlier you expect him to make a reasonable recovery. Are you changing your mind now?"

"No, but…" Again, she hesitated, bound by patient confidentiality, yet aware that as his son, Niko had the right to some information, especially if her withholding it might have an adverse effect on Pavlos's future well-being. "How much do you know about your father's general health?"

"Only what he chooses to tell me, which isn't very much."

She should have guessed he'd say that. *There's no need to contact my son*, Pavlos had decreed, when the hospital had insisted on listing his next of kin. *He minds his business, and I mind mine.*

Niko pinned her in that unnerving green stare. "What aren't you telling me, Emily? Is he dying?"

"Aren't we all, to one extent or another?"

"Don't play mind games with me. I asked you a straightforward question. I'd like a straightforward answer."

"Okay. His age is against him. Although he'd never admit it, he's very frail. It wouldn't take much for him to suffer a relapse."

"I can pretty much figure that out for myself, so what else are you holding back?"

Pavlos spared her having to reply. "What the devil are the pair of you whispering about?" he inquired irascibly.

Casting Niko an apologetic glance, she said, "Your son was just explaining that you might not care for the new bed he ordered. He's afraid you'll think he was interfering."

"He was. I broke my hip, not my brain. I'll decide what I do and don't need."

"Not as long as I'm in charge."

"Don't boss me around, girl. I won't put up with it."

"Yes, you will," she said equably. "That's why you hired me."

"I can fire you just as easily, and have you on a flight back to Vancouver as early as tomorrow."

Recognizing the empty threat for what it really was, she hid a smile. Exhaustion and pain had taken their toll, but by morning he'd be in a better frame of mind. "Yes, sir,

Mr. Leonidas," she returned smartly, and swung the wheel-chair toward the bedroom. "Until then, let me do my job."

Niko had seized the first opportunity to vacate the premises, she noticed, and could have slapped herself for the pang of disappointment that sprouted despite her best efforts to quell it. The faithful Georgios, however, remained on the scene, anxious and willing to help wherever he could. Even so, by the time Pavlos had managed a light meal and was settled comfortably for the night, darkness had fallen.

Damaris, the housekeeper, showed Emily upstairs to the suite prepared for her. Decorated in subtle shades of ivory and slate-blue, it reminded her of her bedroom at home, although the furnishings here were far grander than anything she could afford. Marble floors, a Savonnerie rug and fine antiques polished to a soft gleam exemplified wealth, good taste and comfort.

A lady's writing desk occupied the space between double French doors leading to a balcony. In front of a small blue-tiled fireplace was a fainting couch, its brocade upholstery worn to satin softness, its once-vibrant colors faded by time. A glass-shaded lamp spilled mellow light, and a vase of lilies on a table filled the room with fragrance.

Most inviting of all, though, was the four-poster bed, dressed in finest linens. Almost ten thousand kilometers, and over sixteen hours of travel with its inevitable delays, plus the added stress of her patient's condition, had made serous inroads on her energy, and she wanted nothing more than to lay her head against those snowy-white pillows, pull the soft coverlet over her body and sleep through to morning.

A quick glance around showed that her luggage had been unpacked, her toiletries arranged in the bathroom and her robe and nightshirt laid out on the bench in front of the vanity. But so, to her dismay, was a change of underwear, and a freshly ironed cotton dress, one of the few she'd brought with her, hung in the dressing room connecting bathroom and bedroom. And if they weren't indication enough that the early night she craved was not to be, Damaris's parting remark drove home the point in no uncertain terms.

"I have drawn a bath for you, Despinis Tyler. Dinner will be served in the garden room at nine."

Clearly daily protocol in the Leonidas residence was as elegantly formal as the villa itself, and the sandwich in her room, which Emily had been about to request, clearly wasn't on the menu.

The main floor was deserted when she made her way downstairs just a few minutes past nine, but the faint sound of music and a sliver of golden light spilling from an open door halfway down the central hall indicated where she might find the garden room.

What she didn't expect when she stepped over the threshold was to find that she wouldn't be dining alone.

A round glass-topped table, tastefully set for two, stood in the middle of the floor. A silver ice bucket and two cut-crystal champagne flutes glinted in the almost ethereal glow of dozens, if not hundreds, of miniature white lights laced among the potted shrubs lining the perimeter of the area.

And the final touch? Niko Leonidas, disgracefully gorgeous in pale gray trousers and matching shirt, which together probably cost more than six months' mortgage payments on her town house, leaned against an ornately carved credenza.

She was sadly out of her element, and surely looked it. She supposed she should be grateful her dinner companion wasn't decked out in black tie.

"I wasn't aware you were joining me for dinner," she blurted out, the inner turmoil she thought she'd conquered raging all over again at the sight of him.

He plucked an open bottle of champagne from the ice bucket, filled the crystal flutes and handed one to her. "I wasn't aware I needed an invitation to sit at my father's table."

"I'm not suggesting you do. You have every right—"

"How kind of you to say so."

He'd perfected the art of withering pleasantries, she decided, desperately trying to rein in her swimming senses. The smile accompanying his reply hovered somewhere between derision and scorn, and left her feeling as gauche as she no doubt sounded. "I didn't mean to be rude, Mr. Leonidas," she said, her discomfiture increasing in direct proportion to his suave assurance. "I'm surprised, that's all. I assumed you'd left the house. I understand you have your own place in downtown Athens."

"I do—and we Greeks, by the way, aren't big on honorifics. Call me Niko. Everyone else does."

She didn't care what everyone else did. Finding herself alone with him left her barely able to string two words together without putting her foot in her mouth. Resort to calling him Niko, and she'd probably manage to stuff the other one in next to it.

"At a loss for words, Emily?" he inquired, evil

laughter shimmering in his beautiful green eyes. "Or is it the prospect of sharing a meal with me that has you so perturbed?"

"I'm not perturbed," she said with as much dignity as she could bring to bear. "Just curious about why you'd choose to be here, instead of in your own home. From all accounts, you and Pavlos don't usually spend much time together."

"Nevertheless, I *am* his son, and the last I heard, my choosing to spend an evening under his roof doesn't amount to trespassing. Indeed, given the present circumstances, I consider it my duty to make myself more available. Do you have a problem with that?"

Hardly about to admit that she found him a distraction she wasn't sure she could handle, she said, "Not at all, as long as you don't interfere with my reasons for being here."

"And exactly what are those reasons?"

She stared at him. His eyes weren't glimmering with laughter now; they were as cold and hard as bottle-green glass. "What kind of question is that? You know why I'm here."

"I know that my father has become extremely dependent on you. I know, too, that he's a very vulnerable old man who happens also to be very rich."

She sucked in an outraged breath at the implication in his words. "Are you suggesting I'm after his money?"

"Are you?"

"Certainly not," she snapped. "But that's why you're hanging around here, isn't it? Not because you're worried about your father, but to keep an eye on me and make sure I don't get my hooks into him or his bank account."

"Not quite. I'm 'hanging around' as you so delicately put it, to look out for my father because, in his present condition, he's in no shape to look out for himself. If you find my concern offensive—"

"I do!"

"Then that's a pity," he replied, with a singular lack of remorse. "But try looking at it from my point of view. My father arrives home with a very beautiful woman who happens to be a complete stranger and whom he appears to trust with his life. Not only that, she's come from half a world away and signed on to see him through what promises to be a long and arduous convalescence, even though there's no shortage of nurses here in Athens well qualified to undertake the job. So tell me this: if our situation was reversed, wouldn't you be a little suspicious?"

"No," she shot back heatedly. "Before I leaped to unwarranted conclusions or cast aspersions on her professional integrity, I'd ask to see the stranger's references, and if they didn't satisfy me, I'd contact her previous employers directly to verify that she's everything she purports to be."

"Well, no need to foam at the mouth, sweet thing. Your point is well taken and that being the case, I'm prepared to shelve my suspicions and propose we call a truce and enjoy this very fine champagne I filched from my father's cellar. It'd be a shame to waste it."

She plunked her glass on the table so abruptly that its contents surged over the rim with an indignation that almost matched her own. "If you think I'm about to share a drink with you, let alone a meal, think again! I'd rather starve."

She spun on her heel, bent on making as rapid an exit as possible, but had taken no more than two or three steps toward the door before he caught up with her and slammed it closed with the flat of his hand. "I regret that, in looking out for my father's best interests, I have offended you," he said smoothly. "Trust me, I take no pleasure in having done so."

"Really?" She flung him a glare designed to strip paint off a wall. "You could have fooled me. I'm not used to being treated like a petty criminal."

He shrugged. "If I've insulted you, I apologize, but better I err on the side of caution."

"Meaning what, exactly?"

"That my father's been targeted before by people interested only in taking advantage of him."

"He might not be quite so susceptible to outsiders if he felt more secure in his relationship with you."

"Possibly not, but ours has never been a typical father-son relationship."

"So I've been given to understand, but I suggest the time's come for you to bury your differences and stop butting heads. He needs to know you care."

"I wouldn't be here now, if I didn't care."

"Would it kill you to tell him that?"

He gave a snort of subdued laughter. "No, but the shock of hearing me say so might kill *him*."

What was it about the two of them, that they held each other at such a distance, she wondered. "Do either of you have the first idea of the pain that comes from waiting until it's too late to say 'I love you?' Because I do. More often than I care to remember, I've witnessed the grief and regret that tears families apart because time ran out on them before they said the things that needed to be said."

He paced to the windows at the other end of the aptly named garden room whose exotic flowering plants set in Chinese jardinieres must give it the feel of high summer even in the depths of winter. "We're not other people," he said.

"You're not immortal, either." She hesitated, conflicted once again by how much she could say, then decided to plunge in and disclose what she knew, because she wasn't sure she could live with herself if she didn't. "Look, Niko, he'll probably have my head for telling you this, but your father's not just battling a broken hip. His heart's not in very good shape, either."

"I'm not surprised. That's what comes from years of smoking and hard living, but nothing his doctor said was enough to make him change his ways. He's a stubborn old goat."

That much she knew to be true. Pavlos had discharged himself from Vancouver General against medical advice, and insisted on flying back to Greece even crippled as he was, because he refused to put up with the nursing staff's constant monitoring. *They don't let a man breathe,* he'd complained, when Emily tried to talk him into postponing the journey. *I'll be carried out feetfirst if I let them keep me here any longer.*

"Well, the apple doesn't fall far from the tree, Niko. Where this family's concerned, you're both pretty pigheaded."

He swung around and surveyed her across the width of the room; another long, searching gaze so thorough that a quiver shafted through her. He probed too deeply beneath the surface. Saw things she wasn't ready to acknowledge to herself. "Perhaps before *you* start leaping to unwarranted conclusions," he purred, advancing toward her with the lethal grace of a hunter preparing to move in for the kill, "you should hear my side of the story."

"You're not my patient, your father is," she said, backing away and almost hyperventilating at the determined gleam in his eye.

"But isn't modern medicine all about the holistic approach—curing the spirit in order to heal the body, and such? And isn't that exactly what you've been advocating ever since you walked into this room?"

"I suppose so, yes."

"How do you expect to do that, if you have only half the equation to work with? More to the point, what do you stand to lose by letting me fill in the blanks?"

My soul, and everything I am, she thought, filled with the terrible foreboding that unless she extricated herself now from the web of attraction threatening to engulf her, destiny in the shape of Nikolaos Leonidas would take control of her life, and never give it back again. Yet to scurry away like a frightened rabbit was as alien to her nature as taking advantage of Pavlos. So she stood her ground, pushed the irrational presentiment out of her thoughts and said with deceptive calm, "Absolutely nothing."

"Really?" He leaned toward her, dropped his voice another half octave and latched his fingers around her wrist. "Then why are you so afraid?"

She swallowed and ran her tongue over her dry lips. "I'm not," she said.

CHAPTER TWO

SHE was lying. The evidence was there in her hunted gaze, in her racing pulse, so easily and unobtrusively detected when he took her wrist. And he intended to find out why, because for all that he thought he'd remain unmoved by whatever he discovered when he went to meet their flight, the sight of the old man, so brittle and somehow diminished, had hit him with the force of a hammer blow to the heart. They spent little time together, had long ago agreed to disagree and shared nothing in common. But Pavlos was still his father, and Niko would be damned before he'd let some hot little foreign number take him to the cleaners.

Oh, she'd been full of righteous indignation at his suggestion that she wasn't quite the selfless angel of mercy she presented herself to be. He'd hardly expected otherwise. But he'd also seen how indispensable she'd made herself to Pavlos; how successfully she'd wormed her way into his affections. His father had never been a demonstrative man, at least not that Niko could remember. Which had made the way he'd clung to Emily's hand at the airport all the more telling.

If his assessment of her was correct, redirecting her attention would be simple enough. After all, a millionaire in his vigorous prime was surely preferable to one in his dotage. And if he was wrong…well, a harmless flirtation would hurt no one. Of course, when his father figured out what he was up to, he wouldn't like it, but when was the last time he'd approved of anything Niko did?

"You're very quiet suddenly," she said, interrupting the flow of his thoughts.

He looked deep into her dark blue eyes. "Because I'm beginning to think I've judged you too hastily," he answered, doing his utmost to sound convincingly repentant. "But I'm not entirely without conscience. Therefore, if one of us must leave, let me be the one to go."

Ignoring her whimper of protest, he released her, opened the door to leave the room and found himself face-to-face with Damaris. He could not have orchestrated a better exit. Timing, as he well knew in his line of work, was everything. "*Kali oreksi*, Emily," he said, standing back to allow Damaris to carry in a platter loaded with olives, calamari, dolmades, tzatziki and pita bread. "Enjoy your meal."

He was over the threshold before she burst out, "Oh, don't be so ridiculous!"

Suppressing a smile, he swung around. "There is a problem?"

"If having enough food to feed an army is a problem, then yes."

He shrugged. "What can I say? Greeks love to eat."

"Well, I can't possibly do justice to all this, and since I have no wish to offend your father's housekeeper when she's obviously gone to a great deal of trouble…"

"Yes, Emily?"

She grimaced, as if her next words gave her indigestion. "You might as well stay and help me eat it."

He stroked his jaw and made a show of weighing his options. "It would be a pity to let it go to waste," he eventually conceded, "especially as this is but the first of several courses."

For a moment, he thought he'd overplayed his hand. Skewering him with a glance that would have stopped the gods of Olympus in their tracks, she waited until Damaris mopped up her spilled drink, then took a seat at the table and said, "Try not to gloat, Niko. It's so unattractive."

He wasn't accustomed to female criticism. The women he associated with were so anxious to please, they'd have swallowed their own tongues before issuing such a blunt assessment of his shortcomings. That she suffered no such hesitation appealed to him in ways she couldn't begin to imagine. He devoted his entire life to challenging unfavorable odds. And took enormous pleasure in defeating them.

Collecting the wine bottle as he passed, he joined her and topped up their flutes. Nothing like dim lights and good champagne to set the scene for seduction. Raising his glass, he said, "Here's to getting to know one another all over again."

She responded with the merest tilt of one shoulder, took a dainty sip, then helped herself to a little tzatziki and bread.

"Have more," he urged, pushing the tray of mezedes closer.

She selected an olive, but ignored her champagne.

"You don't care for Greek food?"

"I'm not very familiar with it."

"There are no Greek restaurants in Vancouver?"

"Hundreds, and I'm told they're very good. I just don't eat out very often."

"Why is that? And please don't tell me you lack opportunity. Suitors must be lined up at your door, wanting to wine and dine you."

"I'm afraid not. Shift work tends to put a crimp in a nurse's social life."

Right. And you're such a dedicated professional that you never take a night off!

He shook his head in feigned mystification. "What's wrong with Canadian men, to be so easily discouraged? Are they all eunuchs?"

She almost choked on her olive. "Not as far as I know," she spluttered. "But then, I haven't bothered to ask."

"What about your colleagues? As I understand it, hospitals are a hotbed of romance between doctors and nurses."

"The idea that all nurses end up marrying doctors is a myth," she informed him starchily. "For a start, half the doctors these days are women, and even if they weren't, finding a husband isn't particularly high on my list of priorities."

"Why not? Don't most women want to settle down and have children? Or are you telling me you're the exception?"

"No." She nibbled a sliver of pita bread. "I'd love to get married and have children someday, but only if the right man comes along. I'm not willing to settle for just anyone."

"Define 'the right man,'" he said—a shade too abruptly, if her response was anything to go by.

She dropped her bread and stared at him. "I beg your pardon?"

"By what standards do you judge a prospective husband?"

She reached for her glass and took a sip while she considered the question. "He has to be decent and honorable," she finally declared.

"Tall, dark and handsome, too?"

"Not necessarily." She gave another delicate shrug, just enough to cause her dress to shift gently over her rather lovely breasts.

He wished he didn't find it so alluring. "Rich and successful, then?"

"Gainfully employed, certainly. If we had children, I'd want to be a stay-at-home mom."

"If you had to choose just one quality in this ideal man, what would it be?"

"The capacity to love," she said dreamily, her blue eyes soft, her sweet mouth curved in a smile. Outside, the wind tore at the palm trees with unusual strength for September. "I'd want love more than anything else, because a marriage without it is no marriage at all."

Annoyed to find his thoughts drifting dangerously far from their set course, he said flatly, "I disagree. I'd never let my heart get the better of my head."

"Why not? Don't you believe in love?"

"I might have once, very briefly, many years ago, but then she died of a blood clot to the brain. I was three months old at the time."

"You mean your *mother*?" She clapped a distressed hand to her cheek. Her eyes glistened suspiciously. "Oh, Niko, how very sad for you. I'm so sorry."

He wanted neither her sympathy nor her pity, and crushed both with brutal efficiency. "Don't be. It's not as if she was around long enough for me to miss her."

The way she cringed at his answer left him ashamed. "She gave you life," she said.

"And lost hers doing it, something I've been paying for ever since."

"Why? Her death wasn't your fault."

"According to my father, it was." Her glass remained almost untouched, but his was empty. Needing something to deaden a pain he seldom allowed to surface, he refilled it so hurriedly, the wine foamed up to the brim. "She was forty-one, and giving birth at her age to an infant weighing a strapping five kilos put her in her grave."

"A lot of women wait until their forties to have children."

"They don't all die because of it."

"True. But that's still no reason for you to think Pavlos holds you responsible for the tragedy that befell her. After all, she gave him a son and that's not a legacy any man takes lightly."

"You might be a hell of a fine nurse, Emily Tyler, but you're no spin doctor."

Puzzled, she said, "What do you mean?"

"That nothing you can say changes the fact that my father didn't care if he never had a child. All he ever wanted was my mother, and as far as he's concerned, I took her away from him."

"Then he should have seen to it he didn't get her pregnant in the first place—or are you to blame for that, as well?"

"After twenty-one years of marriage without any sign

of a baby, he probably didn't think precautions were necessary. Finish your wine, woman. I don't care to drink alone. It's a nasty habit to fall into."

She took another cautious sip. "I still can't believe that, once his initial grief subsided, having you didn't bring Pavlos some measure of comfort."

"Then you obviously don't know much about dysfunctional families. My father and I have never liked one another. He has always resented me, not just because I cost him his one true love, but because I remained wilfully unimpressed by his wealth and social status."

"I'd have thought he'd find that commendable."

"Don't let misplaced pity for the poor motherless baby cloud your judgment, my dear," Niko said wryly. "I rebelled every step of the way as a child, took great pleasure in embarrassing him by getting into trouble as a teenager and flat-out refused to be bought by his millions when I finally grew up. I was not a 'nice' boy, and I'm not a 'nice' man."

"That much, at least, I do believe," she shot back, leveling a scornful glance his way. "The only part I question is that you ever grew up. You strike me more as someone with a bad case of defiantly delayed adolescence."

This wasn't playing out the way he'd intended. She was supposed to be all willing, female compliance by now, ready to fall into his arms, if not his bed, not beating him at his own game. And his glass was empty again, damn it! "When you've walked in my shoes," he replied caustically, "feel free to criticize. Until then—"

"But I have," she interrupted. "Walked in your shoes, I mean. Except mine were twice as hard to wear.

Because, you see, I lost *both* my parents in a car accident when I was nine, and unlike you, I remember them enough to miss them very deeply. I remember what it was like to be loved unconditionally, then have that love snatched away in the blink of an eye. I remember the sound of their voices and their laughter—the scent of my mother's perfume and my father's Cuban cigars. And I know very well how it feels to be tolerated by relatives who make no secret of the fact that they've been saddled with a child they never wanted."

Flushed and more animated than Niko had yet seen her, she stopped to draw an irate breath before continuing, "I also learned what it's like to have to work for every cent, and to think twice before frittering away a dollar." She eyed his shirt and watch disdainfully. "You, on the other hand, obviously wouldn't know the meaning of deprivation if it jumped up and bit you in the face, and I don't for a moment buy the idea that your father never wanted you. So all in all, I'd say I come out the uncontested winner in this spontaneous pity party."

He let a beat of silence hang heavy in the air before he spoke again, then, "It's not often someone spells out my many shortcomings so succinctly," he said, "but you've managed to do it admirably. Is there anything else you'd like to tell me about myself before I slither behind the wheel of my car and disappear into the night?"

"Yes," she said. "Eat something. You've had too much to drink and are in no condition to drive. In fact, you should be spending the night here."

"Why, Emily, is that an invitation?"

"No," she said crushingly. "It's an order, and should

you be foolish enough to decide otherwise, I'll kick you where it'll hurt the most."

She probably weighed no more than fifty-four kilos to his eighty-five, but what she lacked in size, she more than made up for in spirit. He had no doubt that, given her knowledge of male anatomy, she was more than capable of inflicting serious injury. Which should have deterred him. Instead the thought of fending her off left him so suddenly and painfully aroused that, for the first time, he questioned the wisdom of his plan of attack. *She* was the one supposed to be at *his* mercy, not the other way around, but so far, she remained utterly indifferent to his charms. He, on the other hand, was anything but impervious to hers.

Damaris came back just then to serve spinach-stuffed breast of chicken and ziti, a welcome diversion, which allowed him to wrestle his wayward hormones into submission and redirect his energy into more productive channels. "Why did you allow my father to coerce you into letting him travel, when he's clearly not up to it?" he inquired casually, once they were alone again.

"I did my best to dissuade him," Emily said. "We all did. But the only thing he cared about was coming home to Greece, and nothing anyone said could convince him to wait. I think it's because he was afraid."

"Of dying?"

"No. Of *not* dying in Greece."

That Niko could well believe. Pavlos had always been fanatically patriotic. "So you volunteered to see him safely home?"

"It was more that he chose me. We got to know one another quite well during his hospital stay."

An hour ago, he'd have rated that little morsel of information as yet another sign of her ulterior motives. Now, he didn't have quite the same enthusiasm for the task. Emily the woman was proving a lot more intriguing than Emily the fortune hunter.

To buy himself enough time to reestablish his priorities, he switched to another subject. "What happened to you after your parents were killed?"

"I was sent to live with my father's sister. He was thirty-six when he died, and Aunt Alicia was eleven years older. She and Uncle Warren didn't have children, but they were the only family I had left, so they were more or less stuck with me. It wasn't a happy arrangement on either side."

"They mistreated you?"

"Not in the way you probably mean, but they never let me forget they'd done 'the right thing' by taking me in and would, I think, have found a reason to refuse if they hadn't been afraid it would reflect badly on them. Of course, the insurance settlement I brought with me sweetened the deal by defraying the cost of putting a roof over my head and keeping me fed and clothed for the next nine years."

"What happened then?"

"The summer I graduated high school, I applied to the faculty of nursing, was accepted and moved into a dorm on the university campus at the end of August. I never went 'home' again."

"But at least there was enough insurance settlement left to pay your tuition fees and other expenses."

She shook her head. "I scraped by on scholarships and student loans."

Caught in a swell of indignation he never saw coming, he stared at her. Whatever else his father's sins, he'd never tampered with Niko's inheritance from his mother. "Are you telling me they spent money on themselves, when it should have been held in trust for your education?"

"No, they were scrupulously honest." She started to add something else, then seemed to think better of it and made do with, "The settlement just wasn't very large to begin with, that's all."

Something about *that* answer didn't sit right, either. Wasn't the whole point of insurance to provide adequate recompense to beneficiaries, especially minors? But although the subject bore investigation, he decided now was not the time to pursue it and asked instead, "Do you keep in touch with your aunt and uncle?"

"A card at Christmas about covers it."

"So they have no idea you're here now?"

"No one has," she said. "My arrangement with Pavlos was strictly between the two of us. If my employer knew what I'd done, I'd probably be fired."

Which wouldn't matter one iota, if Niko's first impression of her was correct and she'd set her sights on a much more rewarding prize. What she earned in a year as a nurse wouldn't amount to pocket change if she married his father.

Wondering if she had any idea how potentially damaging her revelation was, he said, "Then why take the risk?"

"Because your father was alone in a foreign country without friends or family to look after him when he was released."

"He had a son. If you'd thought to contact me, I could have been there within twenty-four hours."

"Maybe," she said gently, "he didn't want to bother you."

"So he bothered a perfect stranger instead, even though doing so might end up costing her her job. Tell me, Emily, how do you propose to explain your absence from the hospital?"

"I won't have to. I took a three-month leave of absence and scheduled it to coincide with his discharge."

"A noble gesture on your part, giving up your holiday to look after my father."

"Well, why not? I had nothing else planned."

Except setting aside an hour a day to polish your halo! Struggling to hide his skepticism, Niko said, "All work and no play hardly seems fair. We'll have to see what we can do to change that."

A sudden gust of wind rattled the French doors, making her jump. "Just being here is change enough. If the weather ever clears up, I'm sure Pavlos won't begrudge me the odd day off to see the sights."

"Count on both," he said, recognizing opportunity when it presented itself. "And on my making myself available to act as tour guide."

"That's nice of you, Niko."

No, it's not, he could have told her. Because whatever *her* motives, *his* were anything but pure. And because he'd meant it when he said he wasn't a nice man.

They passed the remainder of the meal in idle conversation, interrupted only by intermittent bursts of rain at the windows, but before coffee was served, she'd run out of things to say and was wilting visibly. Even he, unscrupulous bastard though he undoubtedly was, felt sorry for her. The long transatlantic flight would have been tiring enough, without the added strain of looking after his father. So when she set aside her napkin and begged to be excused, he made no attempt to stop her, but left the table himself and walked her to the foot of the stairs.

"Good night," she murmured.

"*Kali nikhta,*" he returned. "Sleep well."

She was perhaps halfway to the upper landing when a brilliant flash of lightning arrowed through the night. Almost immediately, the electricity failed and plunged the house into darkness.

He heard her startled exclamation and the click of her high heel hitting the edge of the marble step as she stumbled to a halt. "Stay put," he ordered, well aware how treacherous the staircase could be to the unwary. Once, when he was still a boy, a new housemaid had slipped and broken her arm—and that had been in broad daylight. But he'd grown up in the villa; could quite literally have found his way blindfolded anywhere within its walls, and was at Emily's side before she, too, missed her footing.

Just as he reached her, a second bolt of lightning ripped through the night, bleaching her face of color, turning her hair to silver and her eyes into pools as huge and dark as those found in undersea caverns. "What happened?" she whispered, clutching the bannister with one hand as she teetered on the edge of the stair.

Instinctively he pulled her close with an arm around her shoulders. They felt slender, almost childlike to the touch, but the rest of her, pinned warm and sweet against him, was unmistakably all woman. "The lights went out," he said, resorting to the absurdly obvious in an attempt to deflect her attention from the fact that his body had responded to hers with elemental, albeit untimely vigor.

She choked on a laugh. "I pretty much figured that out for myself."

"I expect a power pole was struck."

"Oh," she said faintly, aware as she had to be of her effect on him. Blatant arousal was difficult to hide at such close quarters. "Does it happen often?"

Were they talking about the same thing, he wondered, as his mind fought a losing battle with his nether regions. "No, especially not at this time of year."

"I ought to make sure your father's all right."

"No need," he said, hearing footsteps and noticing the shadow of candle flames flickering over the walls at the rear of the downstairs hall. "Georgios is already on the job. But if it'll ease your mind any, I'll see you as far as your suite, then go check on him myself. Do you know which one you're in?"

"Only that it's blue and cream, with some gorgeous antique furniture, including a four-poster bed."

He nodded, recognizing her description, and keeping one arm looped around her waist, steered her the rest of the way up the stairs, turned right along the landing and felt his way along the wall on his left until he made contact with her door. Pushing it wide, he directed her inside.

The logs in the fireplace had burned down, but enough of a glow remained to fill the room with dim orange light. Enough that when she looked at him, their gazes locked, held prisoner by the sexual awareness, which had simmered between them from the moment they'd first set eyes on each other.

He hadn't meant to kiss her this early in the game, had planned a much more subtle attack, but when she turned within the circle of his arms and lifted her face to his, it was the most natural thing in the world for him to tighten his hold until she was once again pressed against him. The most natural thing in the world to bend his head and find her mouth with his.

CHAPTER THREE

EMILY had been kissed before, many times, but always with some part of her brain able to rate the experience objectively: too slobbery, too bland, too aggressive, too many teeth, too much heavy breathing, not enough tenderness. More often than not, kissing, she'd concluded, was a vastly overrated prelude to romance. Until Niko Leonidas came on the scene, that was, and felled her with a single blow.

Except "blow" was no more the right word to define his effect on her than "kiss" adequately described his action. What he did with his mouth transcended the ordinary and surpassed the divine. Cool and firm, it yet seared her with its heat. Though undemanding, it somehow stripped her of everything—her independence, her focus, her moral compass, even her sense of survival.

Apart from one rash, distinctly forgettable experience, she'd chosen to remain celibate because sex for its own sake held no appeal, and she'd never come close to being in love. But she'd have let him take her there on the floor, if only he'd asked. Would have let him hike up the skirt of her dress and touch her as no other man ever had. For as long as his kiss held her in its spell, she would have let him have his way with her however he wished.

Obviously he did not wish for a fraction of what she was willing to give. Because releasing her, he stepped back and said, rather hoarsely to be sure, "I'll go look in on my father and see about getting some candles up here."

Weak as water, she clutched the back of a nearby chair and nodded. She couldn't have spoken if her life depended on it. Although he'd put a respectable distance between them, she remained trapped in his aura. Her body still hummed. Her breasts ached. Moisture, warm and heavy, seeped between her thighs.

When he turned away, she wanted to cry out that she didn't need candles, she only needed him. But the words remained dammed in her throat and he was gone before she could free them. Dazed, she lowered herself to the chair and waited for him to return.

A brass carriage clock on the mantelpiece marked the passing minutes. Gradually its measured pace restored her racing pulse to near-normal and brought a sort of order to her scattered thoughts. What kind of madness had possessed her, that she'd been ready to give herself to someone she'd known less than a day? He spelled nothing but trouble.

I won't let him in when he comes back, she resolved. I'm out of my league with such a man and don't need the heartbreak an affair with him would bring.

But when a discreet tap at her door signaled his return, all logic fled. Heat shot through her, giving rise to a single exquisite throb of anticipation that electrified her. She couldn't get to him fast enough.

Pulling open the door, she began, "I was beginning to think you'd abandoned—!" then lapsed into morti-fied silence at the sight of Georgios standing there, a lighted silver candelabra in one hand, and a battery operated lantern in the other.

"Niko asked me to bring these, *thespinis*," he informed her politely, "and to tell you that Kirie Pavlos is sleeping soundly."

Rallying her pride, she stood back to let him pass into the room, and mumbled, "Thank you."

"*Parakalo.*" He placed the candelabra on the dresser and handed her the lantern. "I am also to tell you that he has been called away."

"At this hour of the night?" She made no attempt to hide her disbelief.

He nodded. "*Ne, thespinis.* He received an urgent phone call and will most likely be gone for several days."

Oh, the louse! The cowardly, unmitigated rat! Swallowing the anger and humiliation threatening to choke her, she said scathingly, "It must have been some emergency to drag him out in the middle of a storm like this."

Georgios stopped on his way to the door and shrugged. "I cannot say. He did not explain the reasons."

"Never mind. It's not important." *He* wasn't important. She was there to look after the father, not chase after the son.

"Thank you for the candles and flashlight, Georgios. Good night."

"*Kalispera, thespinis.* Sleep well."

Surprisingly she did, and awoke the next day to clear skies and sunshine. Last night's storm was as much a part of the past as last night's kiss.

Pavlos was already up and dressed when she went

downstairs. He sat on the veranda outside his sitting room, gazing out at the garden. A small empty coffee cup and a phone sat on a table at his side. A pair of binoculars rested on his lap.

Catching sight of her, he pressed a finger to his lips, and gestured for her to join him. "Look," he whispered, pointing to a pair of fairly large birds. Pretty, with bluish-gray heads, pearly-pink breasts and brown wings mottled with black, they pecked at the ground some distance away. "Do you know what they are?"

"Pigeons?" she ventured.

He grunted disdainfully. "Turtle doves, girl! Timid and scarce, these days, but they come to my garden because they know they're safe. And those over there at the feeder are golden orioles. Didn't know I was a bird fancier, did you?"

"No," she said, noting the spark in his dark eyes and his improved color. "But I do know you look much better this morning. You must have had a good night."

"Nothing like being on his home turf to cure a man of whatever ails him. Not that that son of mine would agree. Where do you suppose he is, by the way? I thought he might at least stay over, my first night back."

"No. He was called away on some sort of emergency."

"Gone already, eh?" He squared his shoulders, and lifted his chin, a formidable old warrior not about to admit to weakness of any kind. "Off on another hare-brained escapade, I suppose. Doesn't surprise me. Never really expected he'd stick around. Ah well, good riddance, I say. You had breakfast yet, girl?"

"No," she said, aching for him. He could protest all he liked, but she saw past his proud facade to the lonely parent underneath. "I wanted to see how you were doing, first."

"I'm hungry. Now that you're here, we'll eat together." He picked up the phone, pressed a button and spoke briefly with whoever answered. Shortly after, Georgios wheeled in a drop-leaf table set for breakfast for two, and equipped with everything required for what she soon realized was the almost sacred ritual of making coffee. It was prepared with great ceremony over an open flame, in a little copper pot called a briki, and immediately served in thick white demitasses with a glass of cold water on the side.

"No Greek worthy of the name would dream of starting the day without a *flitzani* of good *kafes*," Pavlos declared.

Possibly not, and she had to admit the aroma was heavenly, but the strong beverage with its layer of foam and residue of grounds took some getting used to. She found the fruit and yogurt salad topped with almonds and drizzled with honey and a sprinkling of cinnamon much more enjoyable.

In the days that followed, she also found out that Pavlos had little faith in doctors, rated physiotherapists as next to useless and had no qualms about saying so to their faces. He could be fractious as a child when forced to suffer through the regimen of exercises prescribed to strengthen his hip, and sweet as peach pie if he thought Emily was working too hard.

While he napped in the afternoons, she swam in the pool, walked along the beach or explored the neighborhood, taking particular pleasure in the shops. In the evenings, she played gin rummy or poker with him, even though he cheated at both.

One morning, she was wheeling him along the

terrace after his physiotherapy session when he asked, "Do you miss home?"

She looked out at the flowers in brilliant bloom, at the peacocks strutting across the lawns, the blue arc of the sky and the stunning turquoise sea. Soon the rainy season would come to Vancouver, its chilly southeasterly gales stripping the trees of leaves. People would be scurrying about under a forest of umbrellas where, just few weeks before, they'd been lying on the beaches taking in the last of summer's sunshine. "No," she said. "I'm happy to be here."

"Good. Then you have no excuse for wanting to leave early."

She thought not, either, until the beginning of her second week there, when Niko reappeared as suddenly as he'd left.

"So this is where you're hiding," he said, coming upon her as she sat reading in a wicker love seat on the patio—except they called it a veranda in Greece. "I've been looking everywhere for you."

Though startled, she managed to hang on to her composure enough to meet his glance coolly and reply with commendable indifference, "Why? What do you want?"

Uninvited, he sat down beside her on the sun-warmed cushions. "To ask you to have dinner with me tonight."

The nerve of him! "I don't think so," she said, projecting what she hoped was an air of cool amusement. "You're likely to take off at the last minute and leave me to foot the bill."

"The way I did the other night, you mean?" He grimaced. "Look, I'm sorry about that but—"

"Forget it, Niko. I have."

"No, you haven't. I haven't, either, and nor do I want to. Spend the evening with me, and I'll try to explain myself."

"Whatever makes you think I'm interested in anything you have to say?"

"Because if you weren't, you wouldn't be so ticked off with me. Come on, Emily," he wheedled, inching closer. "Be fair, and at least hear me out before you decide I'm not worth your time."

"I usually play cards with Pavlos in the evening."

"Then we'll make it a late dinner. How is my father, by the way? I stopped by his suite before I came to find you, but he was sleeping."

"He still tires easily, but he's better since he started physiotherapy."

"I'm glad he's on the mend." He glanced at her from beneath his outrageous lashes, stroked his finger down her arm and left a trail of shimmering sensation in its wake. "So what do you say, sweet thing? Do we have a date?"

Resisting him was like trying to trap mist between her hands. "If that's what it takes for you to leave me to read in peace now, I suppose we do. But I won't be free much before ten, after your father's settled for the night."

He edged closer still, a long, lean specimen of masculine grace, handsome as sin, dangerous as hell, and kissed her cheek. "I can wait that long," he said, "but I'm not saying it will be easy."

He took her to a restaurant on the water, about a fifteen-minute drive from the villa. She'd pinned up her hair in a sleek chignon, and wore a black dress she'd bought on sale in a boutique just a few days earlier, and high-heeled black sandals. Simple but beautifully cut, the dress had a narrow draped skirt, strapless bodice, and a shawl lushly embroidered with silver thread. Her only accessory was a pair of dangling vintage silver earrings studded with crystals.

All in all, a good choice, she decided, glancing at her surroundings. Unlike the bougainvillea-draped tavernas she'd seen in the neighborhood, with their paper tablecloths and simple, sometimes crudely constructed furniture, this place gave new meaning to the term stylish sophistication. Crisp linens, a single perfect gardenia at every place setting, deep, comfortable leather chairs, a small dance floor and soft music combined to create an ambience at once elegant and romantic.

They were shown to a window table overlooking a yacht basin. Tall masts rose black and slender against the night sky. Beyond the breakwater, moonlight carved an icy path across the sea to the horizon, but inside the room, candles cast a warm glow over the stark white walls.

Once they'd been served drinks and he'd chosen their meal—noting no prices were listed on the menu, she'd left him to decide what to order—Niko leaned back in his chair and remarked, "You look very lovely tonight, Emily. More like a fashion model than a nurse."

"Thank you. You look rather nice yourself."

Which had to be, she thought, mentally rolling her eyes, the understatement of the century. The superb fit of his charcoal-gray suit spoke of Italian tailoring at its best, and never mind the gorgeous body inside it.

He inclined his head and smiled. "I like your earrings."

"They were my mother's. She loved jewelry and pretty clothes." She touched her fingertip to one crystal pendant, memories of her mother, all dressed up for an evening out, as clear in her mind as if they'd taken place just yesterday. "I still have all her things—her dinner gowns and shoes and beaded handbags."

"Do you use them?"

"Not often. I don't have occasion to."

His gaze scoured her face, meandered down her throat to her shoulders, and it took all her self-control not to shrink into the concealing folds of her shawl. "What a waste," he murmured. "A woman as beautiful as you should always wear beautiful things."

"My mother was the beauty, not I."

"You think?"

"I know," she said, nodding thanks to the waiter as he presented a tray of appetizers. *Mezedes*, she'd learned, were as integral to the evening meal as the main course itself. "And my father was incredibly handsome. They made such a glamorous couple."

"Tell me about them," he said, resting his elbow on the arm of his chair, wineglass in hand. "What were they like—beyond their good looks, that is?"

"Crazy about one another. Happy."

"Socialites?"

"I suppose they were," she admitted, remembering the many times she'd watched, entranced, as her mother prepared for a gala evening on the town.

"What else?"

She stared out at the yachts rocking gently at their moorings. "They wrung every drop of enjoyment from life. They'd dance in the sitting room after dinner, go swimming at midnight in English Bay, dress up in fabulous costumes for Hallowe'en, decorate the biggest tree they could find at Christmas. They were on everyone's guest list, and everyone wanted to be on theirs. And they died much too soon."

Detecting the sadness infecting her memories, he framed his next question in quiet sympathy. "How did it happen?"

"They were on their way home from a party, driving along a road infamous for its hairpin bends. It was raining heavily, the visibility was poor. They were involved in a head-on collision and killed instantly."

Again, his voice grazed her with compassion. "Ah, Emily, I'm sorry."

Aware her emotions swam dangerously close to the surface, she gave herself a mental shake, sat a little straighter in her seat and firmly changed the subject. "Thank you, but it all happened a long time ago, and we're here to talk about you, not me. So tell me, Niko, exactly what frightened you off after that impulsive kiss last week? And please don't say you were too busy checking the main fuse box to find the cause of the power failure, because Georgios already told me you left after receiving a phone call. Had you forgotten you had a previous date, or was I so inept compared to the other women you know that you couldn't wait to escape me?"

"Neither," he said. "I had to go to work."

"You *work*?"

"Well, yes, Emily," he said, laughing. "Don't most men my age?"

"Yes, but you don't seem the corporate type."

"I'm not."

"And it was the middle of the night."

"Right, again."

"So?"

"So I had to prepare to leave Athens at first light, the next day."

"To go where?"

"Overseas."

"How tactfully vague. You'll be telling me next you're involved in smuggling."

"Sometimes I am."

It was neither the answer she was expecting nor one she wanted to hear. Tired of his stonewalling, she threw down her napkin, pushed back her chair and stood up. "If this is your idea of explaining yourself, I've had enough."

"Okay," he said, grabbing her hand before she could bolt, "I delivered some urgently needed supplies to a medical outpost in Africa."

Abruptly she sat down again, her annoyance fading as the implication of his reply hit home. "Are you talking about Doctors Without Borders?"

"In this particular case, yes."

Their waiter came back just then to whisk away the remains of the mezedes and deliver their main course. A dozen questions crowding her mind, she waited impatiently as he made a big production of serving grilled calamari and prawns on a bed of rice. "How did you get there?" she asked, when they were alone again.

"I flew," Niko said.

"Well, I didn't think you walked!"

His mouth twitched with amusement at her acerbic response. "I happen to own a small fleet of aircraft. It comes in handy on occasion."

"Are you telling me you piloted your own plane?"

"In a word, yes."

"Going into places like that can be dangerous, Niko."

He shrugged. "Perhaps, but someone has to do it."

She stared at him, her every preconceived notion of what he was all about undergoing a drastic change. "Where did you learn to fly?"

"After finishing my National Service, I spent five years as a Career Officer with the HAF—Hellenic Air Force. That's when I first became involved in rescue missions. It irked my father no end, of course, that I chose the military over seconding myself to him and his empire."

"Is that why you did it?"

"Not entirely. I loved the freedom of flying. And providing humanitarian aid wherever it's needed struck me as a more worthwhile undertaking than amassing more wealth. How's your calamari, Emily?"

"Delicious," she said, though in truth she'd hardly tasted it. What she was learning about him was far more interesting. "You said a while ago that you own a fleet of aircraft, which I assume means you have more than one."

"Ten in total, and a staff of fifteen. We're a private outfit, on call twenty-four hours a day, seven days a week, and go wherever we're needed, providing whatever kind of help is required. Last month, we joined forces with the Red Cross after an earthquake in northern Turkey left hundreds homeless. The month before, Oxfam International called on us."

"Well, if you care so little for money, how are you able to afford all that? Does Pavlos support you?"

"You ought to know better than to ask such a question," he scoffed. "Even if he'd offered, I'd have starved before I took a single euro from him. And for the record, I never said I didn't care about money. It's a very useful commodity. I just don't care about his."

"Then I don't understand."

"I inherited a sizable fortune from my mother which, to give credit where it's due, Pavlos invested for me. By the time I had access to it at twenty-one, it had grown to the point that I could do pretty much anything I wanted, without having to rely on sponsors. And I chose to use it benefiting those most in need of help." He glanced up and caught her staring. Again. "Why do you keep looking so surprised?"

"Because you told me last week that you're not a nice man, and I believed you. Now I realize nothing could be further from the truth."

"Don't get carried away, Emily," he warned. "Just because I'm not immune to human suffering doesn't make me a saint."

"But you are, I begin to think, a very good man."

Irritably he pushed aside his plate, most of the food untouched. "The wine must have gone to your head. Let's dance, before you say something you live to regret."

She'd have refused if he'd been in any mood to take no for an answer—and if the prospect of finding herself once more in his arms hadn't been more temptation than she could withstand. "All right," she said, and followed him onto the dance floor.

Weaving a path through the others already swaying to the music, he waited for her to catch up with him and extended his hands in invitation. "Come here, sweet thing," he said, and she went.

Whatever resentment she'd harbored toward him had melted away, and left her completely vulnerable to him, all over again. Who could blame her, when the plain fact of the matter was that with a single touch, a glance from those dark green bedroom eyes, he could make a woman forget everything she'd ever learned about self-preservation? That he also turned out to be so thoroughly *decent* merely added to his appeal and made him that much more irresistible.

CHAPTER FOUR

IT FELT good to hold a woman whose curves hadn't been ravaged by malnutrition. Whose bones, though delicate and fine, were not so brittle that he was afraid they'd break at his touch. Whose breasts hadn't withered from bearing too many children she hadn't been able to nourish properly. Who didn't shrink in fear when a man touched her. Who smelled of flowers, not poverty.

"Stop it," he said, inhaling the sweet fragrance of her hair.

"Stop what?"

"Thinking. I can hear your brain working overtime."

"Well, I can't help wondering—"

He pulled her closer, enough for her warmth to melt the block of ice he carried inside, and make him whole again. Whenever he returned from a particularly harrowing assignment, a woman's soothing voice and generous, vital body always helped erase the hopeless misery he never got used to witnessing; the wasted lives, the terror, the shocking evidence of man's inhumanity to man. "Don't wonder, Emily," he said, glad she'd left her shawl at the table, and loving the ivory smoothness of her skin above the top of her strapless dress. "Don't ask any more questions. Forget everything and just be with me in the moment."

"Not easy to do, Niko. You're not who I thought you were."

Sliding his hand down her spine to cup her hip, he pressed her closer still. "I know," he said.

He was worse. Much worse. Not at all the high-minded hero she was painting him to be, but a man on a mission that was far from laudable where she was concerned. Blatantly deceiving her as to his true motives for dating her, at the same time that he used her to assuage his personal torment.

She stirred in his arms and lifted her face so that her cheek rested against his. The whisper of silk against those parts of her he couldn't see or feel inflamed him. "I'm sorry I jumped to all the wrong conclusions about you."

"You didn't," he muttered, fire racing through his belly. "I'm every bit as bad as you first assumed."

"I don't believe you."

They weren't dancing anymore. Hadn't been for some time. While other couples dipped and glided around them in a slow foxtrot, they stood in the middle of the floor, bodies welded so close together that even if she weren't a nurse well acquainted with male anatomy, she had to know the state he was in.

"What I don't understand," she continued, so intent on her thoughts that nothing he said or did seemed able to derail them, "is how you can show such compassion toward strangers, and spare so little for your father."

"I didn't bring you here to talk about my father."

Her hips nudged against him, a fleeting touch that

stoked his arousal to disastrous heights. "And I wouldn't be here at all, were it not for him."

"Thanks for the reminder," he ground out, dancing her back to their table sedately enough for his rampant flesh to subside. "With that in mind, I'd better get you home if you're to be on the job bright and early in the morning."

"Actually I usually don't start work until nine. Pavlos prefers to have Georgios help him bathe and dress, and I join him for breakfast after that."

He picked up her shawl and flung it around her shoulders. The less he could see of her, the better. "Even so, it's growing late."

She nodded sympathetically. "And you're tired."

"Among other things," he replied ambiguously, gesturing to the waiter for the bill.

Outside, the temperature still hovered around twenty degrees Celsius, warm enough for the top to remain down on the BMW. "Rather than having to drive all the way back to Athens after you drop me off, why don't you stay at your father's house tonight?" she suggested, pulling the shawl more snugly around her as he started along the shore road to the villa.

"No," he said, surprising himself because, at the start of the evening, he'd planned to do exactly that. Had had every intention of seducing her; of using her soft loveliness to erase the heart-rending images he'd brought back with him from Africa and, at the same time, prove his original theory that she would sell herself to the highest bidder. After all, she now knew he had money to burn.

But much though he still desired her, he'd lost his taste for using her. And if she was as duplicitous as he'd first suspected, he was no longer sure he wanted to know.

* * *

It was well after one o'clock in the morning. Within its walls, the villa lay smothered in the thick silence of a household at sleep. Except for Emily, who should have been exhausted, but was instead wide-awake and so disappointed she could have cried.

Pacing to the French windows in her suite, she stepped out on the balcony and promptly wished she hadn't. The classical marble statuary in the garden, gleaming white under the moon, was too reminiscent of Niko's stern profile as he'd driven her home; the cool whisper of night air on her skin, too much a reminder of his lips brushing her cheek as he kissed her good-night.

What had happened, that the evening was covered with stardust promise one moment, and over the next? They'd been so close, so attuned to one another when they were dancing. She'd known how aroused he was, had felt an answering tug of desire for him.

She'd thought, when he announced they should leave the restaurant, that after the way he'd held her, he'd at least end the evening on a high note with a kiss to rival the one from the week before. She'd wanted him to, quite desperately in fact, and why not? He'd redeemed himself so completely in her eyes, she was willing to fan the spark of attraction between them and let it take them to the next level. But rather than setting her on fire as she'd hoped, he'd brought her straight back to the villa and walked her to his father's front door.

"Thank you for a lovely evening," she'd said woodenly, hardly able to contain her disappointment.

"My pleasure," he'd replied. "I'm glad you enjoyed it."

Then he'd bestowed that pale imitation of a kiss on her cheek, muttered, "Good night," and raced back to his idling car as if he was afraid, if he lingered, she might drag him into the shrubbery and insist he ravish her.

What a contradiction in terms he was, she decided, turning back into her room. On the one hand, he was all cool suspicion laced with lethal charm and passion when it suited him, and on the other side of the person-ality coin, a reluctant hero and considerate escort more concerned about keeping her out past her bedtime than catering to his own base needs. Either that, or he took masochistic pleasure in keeping the women he dated off balance. And if that was the case, she was better off without him. One temperamental Leonidas at a time was enough.

"Out on the town till all hours of the night with that no-good son of mine, were you?" Pavlos inquired, glaring at her across the breakfast table when she joined him the next morning. "What if I'd needed you?"

"If you had, Georgios knew how to reach me."

"That's beside the point."

"And exactly what point are you making, Pavlos? That I'm under house arrest and not allowed to leave the premises without your permission?"

Ignoring her sarcasm, he said baldly, "You're asking for trouble, getting involved with Niko. Women are nothing but toys to him, created solely for his entertain-ment and pleasure. He'll play with you for as long as you amuse him, then drop you for the next one who catches his fancy. He'll break your heart without a second thought and leave you to pick up the pieces, just like all the others who came before you."

Not about to admit she'd pretty much reached the

same conclusion herself, she said, "I'm a grown woman. I know how to take care of myself."

He scowled. "Not with a man like him, you don't. He's bad news, no matter how you look at it. Take my advice, girl. Stay away from him."

A shadow fell across the floor. "Talking about me again, old man?" Niko stepped through the open French doors.

No custom-tailored Italian suit this morning, she noted, but blue jeans again, and a short-sleeved blue shirt revealing strong, tanned forearms. Not that the packaging counted for much. It was the man inside and his sexy, hypnotic voice that set her heart to palpitating.

Annoyed that he so easily snagged her in his spell, Emily averted her gaze, but his father continued to look him straight in the eye and said, "Know anyone else who fits the description?"

"Can't think of a soul," Niko replied evenly.

"There you have it then." Pavlos thumped his coffee cup down on the table. "Why are you here anyway?"

"To have a word with Emily, and to see how you're coming along."

"You needn't have bothered."

"Obviously not. You're as cantankerous as ever, which I take to be a very good sign that you're recovering nicely."

"And Emily doesn't want to see you."

"Why don't you let her tell me that for herself? Or does the fact that you're paying her to be your nurse entitle you to act as her mouthpiece, as well?"

"Just stop it, both of you!" Emily cut in. "Pavlos, finish your toast and stop behaving badly. Niko, the physiotherapist should be here soon, and I'll be free to talk to you then."

He shook his head. "Afraid I can't wait that long. I have a meeting in the city—"

"Then don't let us keep you," his father growled, snapping open the morning paper and feigning great interest in the headlines. "And whatever you do, don't hurry back."

Niko's face closed, and spinning on his heel, he strode off down the hall. But not before Emily caught the flicker of pain in his eyes that he couldn't quite disguise.

"That," she told Pavlos, "was both cruel and unnecessary."

"Then chase after him and kiss him better."

"An excellent suggestion," she said, pushing away from the table. "Thank you for thinking of it."

Niko had already reached his car when she yanked open the villa's front door. "Niko, wait," she called, running across the forecourt.

He turned at the sound of her voice, but made no move toward her. "If you're here to apologize for my father, save your breath," he informed her curtly. "I'm used to him."

"Well, I'm not," she said. "Look, I don't know why he's in such a foul mood this morning, but for what it's worth, I want you to know that I don't let other people dictate whom I should or should not associate with."

"In this case, you might be better off if you did," he said, once again turning to get into the car. "After all, he's known me all my life which makes him some sort of expert on what I'm all about."

Stepping closer, she stopped him with a hand on his

arm. Although his skin felt warm, the flesh beneath was unresponsive as stone to her touch. Undeterred, she said, "Perhaps I'd have believed that yesterday at this time, but I know better now and it'll take more than your father's say-so to convince me otherwise. So if you're using the scene back there in the house as an excuse to end our friendship, it's not going to happen. Now, what did you want to talk to me about?"

He regarded her broodingly a moment. "Your time off," he eventually admitted.

"Why do you want to know?"

"Why do you think, Emily? I want to see more of you."

Again, the tell-tale lurch of her heart warned her how susceptible to him she was. "Then why the mixed messages last night, Niko?" she asked, deciding to lay her misgivings to rest once and for all. "Do you blow hot and cold with all the women you date, or have you singled me out for special attention?"

He didn't bother to dissemble. Was, indeed, shockingly, hilariously blunt in his reply. "In case you didn't notice, my dear, last night when we were dancing, I was sporting an erection that would have done a stallion proud. That ought to have told you something."

Smothering a burst of laughter, she said with equal candor, "At the time, I thought it did. But after hustling me outside, you either decided I wasn't quite your type after all, or else you lost your nerve."

A flush of indignation stained his finely chiseled cheekbones. "I neither lost my nerve, nor anything else."

"Then why the hasty brush-off?"

"There's a time and a place for everything, Emily, especially seduction. I'm not the sex-in-the-backseat-of-the-car type of guy—which isn't to say I didn't want to take you to bed. But you'd given no indication you'd have welcomed such an overture. Just the opposite, in fact. You never stopped talking."

"If you'd bothered to ask," she said, "I could have told you we weren't as far apart in our thinking as you seem to suppose. I just did a better job of hiding it."

He blinked. "Are you sure you know what you're saying?"

"Very sure. I realized the moment I set eyes on you that the chemistry between us could easily become explosive."

"This isn't the first time you've left me at a loss for words," he said, almost stumbling over his reply, "and I have a sneaking suspicion it won't be the last."

"Well, don't misunderstand me. I'm not saying I'm ready to jump into bed with you, but…"

"But you won't turn me down if I ask you out again?"

"I'll be disappointed if you don't."

He slid his arm around her waist and pulled her to him. "When's the next time you have a few hours off?"

"Later this afternoon, from about three until seven."

"I'll pick you up at three-thirty. Wear something casual—slacks and a light sweater in case you get cold, and bring a camera if you have one. Today, we play at being tourists in the city."

Then he kissed her. Hard and sweet. On the mouth. And made it last long enough that when he finally released her, she had to clutch the top of the car door to keep herself upright.

She'd read the travel brochures and thought she knew what to expect of Athens. Traffic congestion and noise and smog. Ancient, crumbling ruins sitting cheek by jowl with towering new apartment buildings. And overshadowing them all, the Acropolis and the Parthenon. But brochures didn't come close to preparing her for the real thing.

Niko showed up not in the BMW but on a candy-apple-red motor scooter. Helping her onto the passenger seat, he plunked a bright red helmet on her head, fastened the strap, then climbed aboard himself and said, "Hang on tight."

On that note, they were off, zooming through the outskirts of the city, weaving in and out of traffic, zipping up steep hills, along narrow streets and through tiny squares, until suddenly the famous landmarks were everywhere she looked. She should have been terrified at the speed with which they traveled. With anyone else, she undoubtedly would have been. But seated behind him, her front sandwiched against his spine, her arms wrapped around his waist, she felt fearless, confident.

She loved the wind in her face, the aromas drifting from the tavernas, the energy buzzing in the air. Loved the feel of him, all sleek muscle beneath his short-sleeved shirt, and the scent of his sun-kissed skin.

Finally he parked and locked the scooter, then led her through a pedestrian avenue lined with restaurants and cafés, and along a marble path to the top of the Acropolis. Up close, the sheer size and majesty of the Parthenon overwhelmed her. "I can't believe I'm really here, and seeing it for myself," she breathed. "It's amazing, Niko. Magnificent! And the view…!"

She lapsed into silence, at a loss for words. Athens

lay at her feet, a sprawling mass of concrete occasionally interspersed with the green of pine-covered hills.

"Gives a pretty good idea of the layout of the city," Niko agreed, "but if ever my father decides he can get through an evening without you, we'll come back another time, at sunset. Enjoying a bottle of wine and watching the lights come on is equally impressive."

"What surprises me is that it's not nearly as crowded as I thought it would be."

"Because most tourists have gone home and left Athens to those of us who choose to live here. The smart ones, though, know that October is one of the best times to visit."

They spent an idyllic few hours wandering among the ruins, stopping on the way down the hill for iced coffee at a sidewalk café, and visiting a beautiful little church tucked in a quiet square. But although everything she saw left Emily awestruck, it was what Niko brought to the afternoon that left the most indelible impression.

His lazy smile caressed her, hinting at untold pleasures to come. His voice reciting the history of the temples held her mesmerized. The way he took every opportunity to touch her—holding her hand to guide her over the uneven ground as if she were the most delicate, precious thing in the world to him, or looping an intimate arm around her shoulders as he pointed out some distant landmark—filled her with shimmering happiness.

With a casual endearment, a glance, he inspired in her an unsuspected passion and yearning. The blood seethed in her veins. She had never felt more alive; never known such an uprush of emotion.

Too soon it was six o'clock and time to head back to Vouliagmeni. The setting sun slanted across the lawns and the front door stood open when they arrived at the villa. "Are you coming in?" she asked, as he propped the scooter on its kickstand and swung her to the ground.

He shook his head. "No, *karthula*. Why spoil a perfect afternoon?"

"I wish it didn't have to be like that," she said, removing her helmet.

He took it from her, slung it over the handlebars and cupped her face between his hands. "It is what it is, Emily, and what it's always been."

"Well, I find it very sad. It's not—"

He silenced her with a lingering kiss that emptied her mind of everything but the heady delight of his mouth on hers. "Oh," she breathed, when at last it ended.

He lifted his head and stared past her, then, "I think we should try that again," he murmured, and drawing her to him, kissed her a second time at even greater length.

An exclamation—most likely an expletive, judging by its irate tone—shattered the moment, and spinning around, Emily found Pavlos leaning on his walker, silhouetted in the open doorway.

"Wouldn't you know it?" Niko said cheerfully, releasing her. "Caught in the act by my disapproving *patera*. I'd better make myself scarce before he comes after me with a shotgun. I'll call you, Emily. Soon."

A moment later, he was gone, disappearing down the long driveway in a candy-apple-red blur of speed, and taking with him all the joy the afternoon had brought. Because she knew without a shadow of doubt that the reason he'd kissed her a second time had nothing to do with her. He'd done it for the pure pleasure of stirring his father to anger.

Unbidden, and decidedly unwelcome, Pavlos's earlier warning came back to haunt her. *Women are nothing but toys to him, created solely for his entertainment. He'll break your heart and leave you to pick up the pieces, just like all the others who came before you....*

CHAPTER FIVE

PAVLOS wore such an unmistakable told-you-so expression that Emily knew she looked as let down as she felt. Shuffling along beside her as she stalked into the house, he crowed, "Lived down to my expectations, didn't he?"

"You don't know what you're talking about, Pavlos," she informed him curtly, rallying her pride. "I had a fabulous afternoon."

"And I ran a marathon while you were gone!" He elbowed her in the ribs. "Admit it, Emily. He disappointed you."

"If you must know, you both disappoint me. Father and son—grown men at that—taking potshots at each other isn't my idea of adult entertainment. Have you had dinner?"

"No. I waited for you."

"I'm not hungry."

"Ah, girl! Don't let him do this to you. He's not worth it."

The edge of compassion softening his tone caused serious inroads on her composure, and that he happened also to be right didn't make the advice any easier to swallow. "He's not 'doing' anything," she insisted.

Except play fast and loose with her emotions, which she wasn't about to admit to his father.

That night when he was preparing for bed, Pavlos slipped on the marble tiles in his bathroom and split his forehead open on the edge of the sink. Striving to maintain calm in the face of chaos—Georgios panicked at the sight of blood, was sure his beloved master was dying and blamed himself for the accident—Emily directed him to call for an ambulance while she attended to Pavlos who lay sprawled on the floor. Although somewhat disoriented, he swore irritably and smacked her hand away when she tried to prevent him from struggling to his feet.

Leaning against the tub, he scoffed, "I'm not dead yet, woman! It'll take more than a cracked skull to finish me off."

"It's not your head I'm worried about, it's your hip," she said, applying a folded facecloth to the superficial cut on his brow. In fact, the sink had broken his fall and that he was able to sit on the floor without showing much evidence of pain was a good sign, but she wanted more scientific proof that he was as fine as he claimed.

The paramedics arrived shortly after and transferred him to the hospital for X-rays. Fortunately he'd incurred no further damage to his hip, required only a couple of sutures to his cut and vetoed any recommendation that he stay there overnight. "I didn't bring you all this way to look after me so you could turn the job over to some-one else," he reminded Emily.

By the next morning, he sported a black eye but was otherwise his usual self. "No reason to," he snapped, when she suggested letting his son know what had happened.

But, "He has a right to be kept informed," she insisted, and left a brief message on Niko's voice mail.

He didn't acknowledge it until three days later when he again showed up unannounced as they were finishing lunch. "Very colorful," he remarked, inspecting Pavlos's black eye which by then had taken on a distinctly greenish hue. "Tell me, old man, do you plan to make a habit of abusing your body?"

"Accidents happen," his father shot back. "You're living proof of that."

Emily winced, appalled by the stunning cruelty of his reply, but realized that although he'd rather die than admit it, Pavlos was hurt that Niko hadn't bothered to stop by sooner.

"We all have our crosses to bear, *Patero*," Niko said scornfully. "Yours isn't any heavier than mine."

"Don't call me *patero*. You're no more a son to me than a dog on the street."

After their last confrontation, Emily had made up her mind she was never again getting caught in the middle when these two went at each other, but the insults flying back and forth were more than she could tolerate. "How do you the pair of you live with yourselves?" she asked sharply.

"By having as little to do with each other as possible," Niko said, addressing her directly for the first time since he'd entered the room. "*Yiasu*, Emily. How have you been?"

"Very well, thank you. The same can't be said of your father, but I guess that didn't much matter to you, seeing that you waited three days to visit him after his accident."

"Don't waste your breath appealing to his sense of decency," Pavlos advised her. "He doesn't have one."

Niko regarded him with weary disdain. "Unlike you in your prime, my career involves more than sitting behind a desk while my minions do all the work. I was away on assignment and didn't get back to Athens until this morning."

"Racing off on another mercy mission to save the world, were you?" Pavlos sneered.

"As to *thialo, yarro!*"

"You hear that, Emily?" Pavlos flung her an injured glare. "He told me to go to hell!"

Emily glanced from one to the other. At the father, his iron-gray hair still thick and his eyes piercingly alive, but his once-powerful body decaying, its bones so brittle it was a miracle they hadn't crumbled when he fell. At the son, a modern-day Adonis, tall, strong and indomitable. And both so proud, they'd have walked barefoot through fire rather than admit they cared about each other.

"I can't imagine why he bothered," she said witheringly. "The way I see it, he's already there, and so are you."

On that note, she left them. They might be determined to tear one another apart, but she'd be damned if she'd stay around to pick up the pieces.

Exiting through the French doors, she marched along the terrace and around the side of the villa to the lodge behind the garages. The widowed gardener, Theo, and his son, Mihalis, whom she'd met the day she arrived, lived there. Snoozing on the step outside the back door was their dog, Zephyr, a big friendly creature of indeterminate breed who, when she approached, wriggled over to make room for her to sit beside him and planted his head on her lap.

Niko found her there a few minutes later. "Is there space down there for me, too?"

"No," she said. "I prefer civilized company and you don't qualify."

"But the dog does?"

"Definitely. I'll take him over you any day of the week."

He shoved his hands in the back pockets of his jeans and regarded her moodily. "For what it's worth, Emily, I take no pleasure in constantly doing battle with my father."

"Then why don't you put an end to it?"

"What would you have me do? Stand by and let him use me as a verbal punching bag?"

"If that's what it takes…"

"Sorry, *karthula*, I'm not the subservient type. And I'm not here now to carry on with you where I left off with him."

"Why are you here, then?"

"To ask if you'll have dinner with me again."

"What for? So you can flaunt me in your father's face, the way you did the other day?"

Ignoring Zephyr's warning growl, he hunkered down on the few inches of sun-warmed step beside her. "Would you believe because I can't stay away from you, though heaven knows I wish I could?"

"Why? Because you blame me for your father's accident?"

"Don't be absurd," he said. "Of course I don't."

"Perhaps you should. I'm supposed to be nursing him back to health, not exposing him to further injury.

It's a miracle he didn't do more damage to himself when he fell."

"The point is, he didn't, and I knew it within hours of the accident."

"How is that possible if, as you claim, you arrived back in town only this morning?"

"This might come as a surprise, Emily, but I'm not completely heartless. I admit I'm away more often than I'm here, but I maintain regular contact with Georgios or Damaris, and know practically to the minute if a problem arises. Judging from their glowing reports, not only are you a dedicated and skilled professional who's taking excellent care of Pavlos, but you're earmarked for sainthood when you die—which, I hasten to add, I hope won't be anytime soon."

"If you care enough about him to phone them for an update on how he's doing, would it hurt you to tell him so?"

"Why would I bother when he makes it patently clear it's not something he wants to hear?"

"He might surprise you."

"You're the only one to surprise me, Emily, and I can't say I'm enjoying the experience. I've got enough on my mind, without that."

At his gloomy tone, she ventured a glance at him. Noticed the grim set of his mouth, the frown puckering his brow and felt an unwelcome stab of sympathy. "You ran into problems when you were away?"

"Nothing unusual about that," he said, shrugging. "My business is all about solving problems, as long as they're other people's. But I learned a long time ago that the only way to deal effectively with them is to draw a firm line between my work and my personal life, the latter of which I make a point of keeping complication free." He paused, sketched a groove in the dust with the toe of his shoe as if to illustrate his point and laced his fingers through hers. "But somehow, you've become just that, Emily. A complication. One I can't ignore."

"I don't see how."

"I know you don't. That's half the trouble."

"Try explaining it, then."

"I can't," he said morosely. "That's the other half."

She sighed, exasperated, and pulled her fingers free. "I'm not a big fan of riddles, Niko, and you don't appear exactly overjoyed to be involved with me, so let me put us both out of our misery. Thanks, but no thanks. I don't want to have dinner with you again."

Bathing her in a molten-green gaze, he inched closer. Slid his hand around her nape. "Liar," he murmured, the tip of his tongue dallying insolently with the outer curve of her ear.

The last time a man had tried that, she'd barely managed to suppress a revolted *Eeuw!* before she shoved him away. What was so different about Niko Leonidas, that his every touch, every glance, left her panting for more?

"Just because I refuse to let you play games with me doesn't make me a liar," she insisted weakly, almost paralyzed by the throb of tension unwinding inside her to affect body parts she was beginning to wish she didn't have.

"It doesn't make you any easier to resist, either."

"Then I guess we've reached an impasse."

For a long moment, he stared at her as if trying to fathom the solution to a dilemma only he could resolve.

Then with a shrug that plainly said, *Ah, to hell with it,* he rose to his feet with indolent grace. "I guess we have," he replied, and sauntered away.

"Good riddance!" she muttered, crushing the wave of disappointment threatening to engulf her. "Other women might trip over themselves in their eagerness to fall in with your every whim and wish, but I'm made of sterner stuff."

She repeated her little mantra several times during the rest of the afternoon, because it was all that stood between her and the urge to call him and say she'd changed her mind about spending the evening with him. To make quite sure she didn't weaken at the last minute, she went for a long walk on the beach, and ate dinner at a taverna. Upon her return to the villa, she played checkers with Pavlos for an hour, then pleading a headache, escaped to her suite.

Night had long since fallen, and closing the door behind her, she surveyed her sanctuary with a mixture of relief and pleasure. Damaris had turned back the bed-covers and made a fire against the chill of mid-October. Flames danced in the hearth and cast burnished-gold reflections over the polished antique furniture. The pleasant scent of burning olive wood filled the air.

Yes, she'd definitely made the right decision, Emily thought, tossing her sweater on the foot of the bed and kicking off her shoes. Although she couldn't deny the magnetic attraction between her and Niko, she couldn't ignore her feminine intuition, either. From the start, it had warned her that giving in to her attraction to him would invite nothing but trouble. If she didn't step back now, she'd find herself hopelessly, helplessly entangled with a man so far out of her league that she'd be guaranteed nothing but misery. After all, he'd made it graphically clear that his interest in her was purely sexual, and realistically, what else could she expect? He had no room in his life for a serious relationship, and even if he had, her future lay half a world away.

Warding off the unavoidable but depressing truth of the matter, she went into the bathroom and while the whirlpool tub filled, stripped off the rest of her clothes, pinned up her hair and lit a scented candle. Solitude was preferable to heartache any day of the week, she told herself bracingly, as she sank up to her chin in the hot water and let the air jets massage the day's tension into oblivion.

With the candle finally burned down to nothing, she dried herself with a towel from the heated rack, applied a generous dollop of body lotion to her water-wrinkled skin and pulled on a clean nightshirt. Then feeling limp as cooked spaghetti and so relaxed it was all she could do to stand upright, she tottered back to her bedroom.

Surprisingly the fire still burned brightly as if it had recently been replenished. And her shoes stood neatly aligned next to the armchair which, she noticed in appalled disbelief, was occupied. By Niko.

"I was beginning to think you'd drowned," he remarked conversationally.

Horribly aware that she wore nothing but a nightshirt whose hem came only midway down her thighs, she tried ineffectually to tug it lower. A huge mistake because, when she let it go, it sprang up with alarming vigor and revealed heaven only knew what of her anatomy. "Don't look!" she squeaked, shock rendering her incapable of a more quelling response.

"If you insist," he said, and very politely turned his head aside.

"How did you get in here?"

"Through the door, Emily. It seemed the most logical route to take."

If she had an ounce of backbone, she'd have matched his sarcasm and told him to leave the same way, but curiosity got the better of her. "Why?"

"I decided I owe you an explanation. Again!"

Wishing the sight of him didn't fill her with such desperate yearning that she was practically melting inside, she said, "You don't owe me anything, Niko. And you have no business being in my room."

"But I'm here regardless, and I'm staying until I've had my say."

"It seems to me we've been through this routine before and it got us precisely nowhere."

"Please, Emily."

She gave a long suffering sigh. "Then make it quick. I'm tired and I want to go to bed."

He slewed an audacious glance at her bare legs. "Could you put on something a little less revealing first? I'm only human, and staring at the fire doesn't quite cut it compared to looking at you."

Annoyed at the burst of pleasure his words aroused, she stomped back into the bathroom, grabbed the full length robe hanging on the door and dived into it.

"That's better," he said, vacating the armchair when she returned with only her hands, feet and head open to his inspection. "Why don't you sit here?"

"No, thanks," she informed him starchily. "I don't anticipate this taking very long."

He'd convinced himself this would be easy. All he had to do was reiterate his initial reservations, explain he'd put them to rest and no longer had ulterior motives for pursuing her. But the sight of her when she first came out of the bathroom had wiped his mind clean of anything but the raging desire to touch her all over. To lift that absurd scrap of a nightgown and bury his mouth at the cluster of soft, silver-blond curls she'd so briefly and tantalizingly revealed in her attempt at modesty.

"I'm waiting, Niko," she reminded him, sounding like his high school math teacher.

Would that she looked like her, too—moustache and all! "I want to start afresh with you," he said.

"I'm not sure I understand what that means."

He swallowed, grasping for the words that persisted in eluding him. "We got off on the wrong foot, Emily. You're my father's nurse, and I'm his son...."

"To the best of my knowledge, the status quo hasn't changed. I'm still his nurse. You're still his son."

How could he do it? How cut to the chase and say bluntly, *Despite pretending I no longer believed it, I remained convinced you were out to take him for all he's worth and decided my only choice was to seduce you, but have now decided I was wrong,* and expect her to understand? He wouldn't, if their situation were reversed.

"But something else *has* changed," he said instead.

"What?"

He took a deep breath and plunged in, laundering the

truth in a way that made him cringe inside. "Can we just say I'm tired of playing games and leave it at that? I'm not interested in using you to score points off my father, or for any other reason. I want to be close to you not because it'll annoy him to see us together, but because I like you for yourself. So I guess the only questions still to be answered are, do you want the same thing, or have I misread the signs and the attraction I thought existed between us is just a figment of my imagination?"

"It's not a figment of your imagination," she admitted, "but I don't understand why you'd pursue it when you said just this afternoon that I was a complication you didn't need."

"Overanalyzing is second nature to me. It's saved my skin more often than I care to count. But in this case, I took it too far."

She shifted from one foot to the other, clearly weighing his words. "Maybe not," she said judiciously. "Maybe you simply realized there was no future in a relationship with me."

"Never counting on the future is another by-product of my job. The only certainty is the here and now."

He took a step toward her, then another, until he was close enough to inhale the scent of her skin. She'd pinned up her hair, but tendrils had escaped to curl damply against her neck. The robe was at least two sizes too large and gaped at the front, drawing his gaze to the faint swell of her cleavage just visible above the top of her nightshirt.

The urge to kiss her, to hold her, nearly blinded him. "What do you say, Emily?" he asked hoarsely. "Will you take a chance on it with me?"

CHAPTER SIX

THE persistent voice of caution warned her not to fall for his line of reasoning. What was he offering her, after all, but the pleasure of the moment?

On the other hand, what had she gained in the past by pinning all her hopes on a better tomorrow? A degree in nursing, a crippling mortgage on her town house, a secondhand car and a short-lived, disappointing relationship with a medical student. Even her circle of friends had dwindled as more and more of them exchanged the single life for marriage and babies. Not that they completely abandoned her, but their interests no longer coincided as they once had. Her schedule revolved around shift work and case histories; theirs, around spouses and midnight feedings.

"Emily?" Niko's voice flowed over her, sliding inside the bathrobe supposedly shielding her from his potent appeal, to caress every hidden inch of skin, every minute pore.

Why was she holding out for a future that might never dawn, when the man who epitomized her every waking fantasy was offering her the chance to fulfill them? Giving in to her heart instead of her head, she lifted her gaze to meet his and whispered, "Why don't you stop talking and just kiss me?"

He groaned and reached for her. Cupped her face between his hands and swept his lips over her eyelids, her cheekbones, her jaw. And finally, when she was quivering all over with anticipation, he buried his mouth against hers. Not as he had before, with calculated finesse, but in scalding, desperate greed.

For the first time in her life, her natural caution deserted her, annihilated by a yearning so painful, she was filled with the consuming need to satisfy it at any price. Barely aware that she'd anchored her arms around his waist, she tilted her hips so that they nudged boldly against him exactly where he was most evidently aroused. His hard, unabashed virility inflamed her, scorching any remnant of doubt to ashes.

Somehow, her robe fell undone and he was touching her, his clever seeking fingers tracing a path from her collarbone and inside her sleeveless nightshirt to shape the curve of her breast. But she wanted more and tried to tell him so, angling herself so that her nipple surged against his palm, and pleading with him not to stop.

But stop he did. "Not here," he ground out, a sheen of sweat glistening on his brow. "Not in my father's house."

"But I can't leave," she whimpered. "What if he needs me and I'm not here?"

"Emily, *I* need you. I need you now."

Without a twinge of shame, she lifted the hem of her nightshirt and guided his hand between her legs. "You think I don't need you just as badly?"

Chest heaving, he molded his hand against her and pressed, flexing his fingers just so. The ensuing jolt of sensation ricocheted through her body and almost brought her to her knees. Gasping, she sank against him.

Steering her backward, he lowered her to the bed and touched her again, teasing the pivotal nub of flesh at her core that marked the dividing line between cool reason and clamoring ecstasy. And when she tipped over the edge in explosive release, he smothered her high-pitched cry with his mouth and stroked her until the spasms racking her body faded to an echo.

How many languid minutes ticked by before he pushed himself upright and, in a belated attempt to restore her modesty, covered her limbs with the bathrobe? Not nearly enough, and she clung to him. "Stay," she begged.

He shook his head. "I can't."

"Don't you want me, Niko?"

"So badly I can taste it. But not with my father's shadow hanging over us."

"Then how…when…?"

"Tell him you're taking the weekend off. We'll go away to someplace where we can be completely alone."

"What if he won't agree?"

"He doesn't own you, *karthula*," he said. Then, searching her face, asked, "Or does he?"

"Of course not, but he *is* my patient and he *is* paying me to look after him. And whether or not you accept it, he isn't as far along the road to recovery as he'd have you believe. To expect Georgios to assume responsibility for him would be unprofessional and negligent on my part."

"All it takes to solve that problem is a phone call to a private nursing agency for someone to replace you.

We're talking three days at the most. He can manage without you for that short a time."

"I suppose," she acknowledged dubiously, not because she wasn't sure she wanted to spend the weekend with him, but because she knew she'd have to fight Pavlos to get it.

A muscle twitched in Niko's jaw. "You know, Emily, if I'm asking too much—"

"You're not!"

"Are you sure?"

"Yes." She pressed her lips together and nodded. For pity's sake, when had she turned into such a wimp? She'd been in Greece over three weeks and more or less at Pavlos's beck and call the entire time. It wasn't unreasonable for her to ask for a break. "I'll work something out, I promise."

He brushed a last kiss over her mouth. "Let me know when it's arranged."

In the hectic two days that followed, she alternated between euphoria and bouts of horror at how shamelessly she'd offered herself to Niko. How would she ever face him again? But her yearning outweighed her chagrin and overriding Pavlos's objections, she booked the weekend off.

"A bikini and lots of sunscreen," Niko said, when she called to tell him she'd be ready to leave on Friday evening at six and asked what she should pack.

"What else?"

She could almost hear his shrug. "Something warm for the evenings, maybe, although the weather's supposed to be good. Shorts, a couple of tops. Not enough to fill a suitcase, by any means. Just throw a few things in a carryall."

"In other words, travel light and keep it casual."

"That about covers it, yes."

Much he knew, she thought, scurrying out to shop late Thursday afternoon while Pavlos napped. The clothes she'd brought with her to Greece were, for the most part, serviceable and basic. She hadn't come on vacation, she'd come to work, and in her profession that meant easily laundered cotton slacks and tunic tops, and comfortable, soft-soled shoes. She certainly didn't have anything designed for a romantic weekend with the sexiest man on the planet.

After dinner that night, she laid out her purchases, setting aside the dark red velour jogging suit and white socks and runners for traveling, but stuffing racy new lingerie, sheer nightgown, sandals and silk caftan, as well as shampoo, toothbrush, cosmetics and all the other items he'd specified, into a canvas tote designed to hold far less. He had said they'd be completely alone, but clearly didn't understand that it wasn't looking the part for strangers that she cared about, it was looking her best for him.

Although Pavlos had allowed a nurse from an agency to fill in for her while she was gone, he'd made it plain he was doing so under duress. To drive home the point, he sulked all Friday morning and ignored Emily all afternoon.

The one thing he hadn't done was inquire where she was going, or with whom, although from his dire mutterings, he'd obviously concluded it somehow involved Niko. So with her replacement up to speed on her duties, and rather than starting the weekend on a sour note with a confrontation, Emily collected her bag and slipped out of the villa a few minutes before six, to wait for Niko at the foot of the driveway.

Right on time, he drew up in the BMW. "You made it," he greeted her, slinging his arm around her shoulders in a brief hug.

"Did you think I wouldn't?"

"Let's just say I wouldn't have been surprised if my father had thrown himself on the floor and started foaming at the mouth when you tried to leave. And the fact that you're lurking here, hidden from view by anyone in the villa, tells me you pretty much feared the same."

"If I admit you're right, can we agree that the subject of your father is off-limits for the duration of the weekend?"

"Gladly." He tossed her bag in the trunk and held open the passenger door. "Hop in, Emily. I want to get underway while we still have some daylight left."

"Underway," she discovered was not aboard an aircraft as she'd half expected, but a fifty-two-foot sloop moored at a private yacht club in Glyfada, a twenty-five minute drive north of Vouliagmeni. Sleek and elegant, with a dark blue hull and the name *Alcyone* painted in gold across her transom, she was, Niko told Emily, built for speed. But without any wind to fill her sails and sunset no more than a crimson memory on the horizon, he was forced to steer her under diesel power to the tiny island of Fleves, just off the east coast of the Attic peninsula.

It was a short trip only, but what made it magical for Emily was the rising moon, which laid down a path of silver to mark their passage, and the luminescence sparkling in their wake like a handful of tiny diamonds.

Niko, in blue jeans and a lightweight cream sweater wasn't too hard to take, either.

After they'd dropped anchor, he set a lantern over the companionway in the center cockpit, told her to stay put and disappeared below, returning a few minutes later with a bottle of chilled white wine, crystal glasses and a small tray of appetizers. "I'd toast you in champagne," he said, taking a seat across from her and pouring the wine, "but it doesn't travel well in a sailboat."

"I don't need champagne," she assured him. "I'm happy just to be here with you."

He tipped the rim of his glass against hers. "Then here's to us, *karthula*."

The wine dancing over her tongue, crisp and cold, lent her courage. "You've called me that before. What does it mean?"

"Sweetheart." He raised one dark brow questioningly. "Do you mind?"

"No," she said, and shivered with pleasure inside her cozy velour jogging suit.

Noticing, he gestured below deck. "Dinner's in the oven and should be ready soon, but we can sit in the cabin where it's warmer, if you like."

"I'd rather not," she said, shying away from the closed intimacy it presented. Now that the rush and excitement of getting away was over and it was at last just the two of them, she was gripped with an almost paralyzing shyness. "It's so peaceful and quiet on deck."

"But you're on edge. Why is that, Emily? Are you wishing you hadn't agreed to spend the weekend with me?"

"Not exactly. I'm just a little…uncomfortable."

He scrutinized her in silence a moment, tracking the conflicting emotions flitting over her face. At last, he said, "About us being here now, or about the other night?"

She blushed so fiercely, it was a miracle her hair didn't catch fire. "Do we have to talk about the other night?"

"Apparently we do," he said.

She fiddled with her glass, twirling it so that the lantern light glimmered over its surface. From the safety of distance, she'd been able to put her conduct on Wednesday down to a temporary madness *he'd* inspired. But now, with no means of escaping his probing gaze, how she'd responded to him left her feeling only shamefully wanton and pitifully desperate.

What had possessed her to behave so completely out of character? Professionally she was ICU Nurse Tyler, capable, skilled and always in control. Socially, she was good friend Emily, affable, dependable—but again, always in control.

She did not rush headlong into affairs, she did not beg a man to make love to her and she most certainly did not brazenly invite him to explore her private parts. That she had done all three with Niko made her cringe. Yet, here she was, because embarrassed or not, she couldn't stay away from him. And that meant facing up to what had transpired between them.

"You must know how very difficult it was for me to leave you as I did," he said softly, divining so exactly the source of her discomfort that she wondered if she'd actually voiced her thoughts aloud. "I won't pretend I'm not eager to pick up where we left off, but only if you feel the same. We take this at your pace, Emily, or not at all."

She glanced around, at the velvet moonlit night; at the dark hulk of the island rising to her left. She listened to the silence, broken only by the gentle wash of the sea against the boat's hull. Finally she dared to look at the man staring at her so intently. "It's what I want, too," she admitted. "I'm just a little out of my element. This is all very new to me, Niko."

His posture changed from indolent relaxation to sudden vigilance. "Are you trying to tell me you're a virgin?"

She choked on her wine. "No."

"No, that's not what you're trying to tell me, or no, you're not a virgin?"

"That's not what I'm trying to tell you. I was referring to the setting—the boat, the glamour, the exotic location. As for whether or not I'm a virgin, does it really matter?"

"Yes, it does," he said soberly. "Not because I'll judge you one way or the other, but because if I'm your first lover, I want to know beforehand." He leaned across and touched her hand. "So?"

Another blush raced up her neck to stain her face, though she hoped it didn't show in the dim light. "I'm not."

Picking up on her discomfiture anyway, he burst out laughing. "Don't look so mortified," he said. "I'm not, either."

"But it was only once, and not exactly…a howling success. Contrary to the impression I might have given you the other night, I'm not very good at…well…*this*."

"I see," he said, making a visible effort to keep a straight face. "Well, now that you've got that off your chest, what do you say we have dinner and let the rest of the evening take care of itself?"

"I'd like to freshen up first." In reality, she'd like to put her head down the toilet and flush, or better yet, jump over the side of the boat and never resurface.

"Sure," he said easily. "I'll be a couple of minutes getting everything ready, so take your time. Our stuff's in the aft cabin, which has its own bathroom."

It had its own built-in king-size bed, too. Dressed in navy-blue linens, with a wide ledge and window at the head, and brass wall lamps on either side, it set the stage for seduction and sent a tremor of terrified anticipation fluttering in Emily's stomach.

Would she disappoint him? she wondered, unpacking her clothes and laying out her toiletries on the vanity in the bathroom. Make an even bigger fool of herself this time than she had before? Was she being too reckless, too naive, in straying so far out of her usual comfort zone? Or had she finally found the one man in the world who made all the risks of falling in love worthwhile?

Soft lights and music greeted her when she returned to the main cabin. The air was fragrant with the scent of oregano and rosemary. Navy-blue place mats and napkins, crystal, brushed stainless steel cutlery and white bone china graced the table. In the galley, on the counter above the refrigerator, were a basket of bread and a bowl containing olives, and chunks of tomato, cucumber and feta cheese drizzled with olive oil.

Long legs braced against the barely perceptible rise and fall of the boat, Niko stood beside the oven, arranging skewers of roasted lamb, eggplant and peppers over rice. "Not exactly a gourmet spread," he remarked, carrying the platter to the table. "Just plain, simple picnic fare."

"I'd hardly call it plain or simple," she said, thinking of the plastic forks and paper plates, which marked the picnics she usually attended. "How do you keep your dishes and glassware from breaking when you're under sail?"

"I had the boat custom built with cabinetry designed to keep everything safely in place. I'll show you later, if you're interested."

"Interested? Intrigued is more like it. At the risk of repeating myself, you're not at all the playboy I took you to be when I first met you."

Green eyes filled with amusement, he said, "You're an expert on playboys, are you?"

"No, but I'm willing to bet they don't put their lives on the line to help people in distress, and they don't cook."

"Don't let the meal fool you. I had it prepared at a local taverna. All I had to do was heat up the main course, which pretty much sums up my talents in the kitchen."

He brought the bread and salad to the table, poured more wine and clinked his glass against hers. "Here's to us again, *karthula*. Dig in before everything gets cold."

The food was delicious; conversation easy and uncomplicated as they discovered more about each other. They both enjoyed reading and agreed they could live without television as long as they had a supply of good books at hand, although he preferred nonfiction whereas she devoured novels. And neither could live without a daily newspaper.

Niko was an avid scuba diver and had explored a

number of wrecks off the Egyptian coast. The best Emily could manage was snorkeling in a protected lagoon and admitted to being nervous if she was too far away from the shore.

He'd seen parts of the world tourists never visited. She stayed on the safe and beaten track: other parts of Canada, Hawaii, the British Virgin Islands.

When they'd finished eating, she helped him clear the table. Dried the dishes he washed. Stacked the wineglasses in the cunning little rack designed to hold them. And loved the domesticity of it all. A man, a woman, a nest...

As ten o'clock inched toward eleven, he suggested they finish their wine on deck. The moon rode high by then, splashing the boat with cool light, but he took a blanket from a locker and wrapped them both in its fleecy warmth.

"I dream about places like this when I'm away," he said, pulling her into the curve of his arm. "It's what keeps me sane."

"What is it about your work that made you choose it? The thrill, the danger?"

"In part, yes. I'd never find satisfaction playing the corporate mogul sitting behind a mile-wide desk and counting my millions, despite my father's trying to buy my allegiance with more money than I could spend in a century of profligate living. To him, money's the ultimate weapon for bringing a man to heel, and it infuriated him that, in leaving me my own fortune, my mother stripped him of that power over me. It's the one thing she did that he resented."

"But there's another reason you decided on such an unconventional career?"

He shifted slightly, as if he suddenly found the luxuriously padded seat in the cockpit uncomfortable. "This isn't something I'd tell to just anyone, but yes, there's another reason. Using her money to help people in need eases my conscience at having killed her."

Aghast to think he'd carried such a heavy burden of guilt all his life, Emily burst out, "I know I've said this before, but her death was an unforeseen tragedy, Niko, and you're too intelligent a man to go on blaming yourself for something that wasn't your fault. That Pavlos let you grow up believing otherwise—"

"I thought we'd agreed not to talk about my father."

"We did, but you're the one who mentioned him first."

"Well, now I want to forget him, so let's talk about your parents instead, and satisfy my curiosity on a point that's puzzled me ever since you first mentioned it. You said they were killed in a car accident, so how is it that you were left with virtually no financial security? Usually in such cases, there's a substantial settlement, especially when a minor is left orphaned."

If she'd pressured him into confronting his own demons, his question very neatly forced her to address her own. "There was no settlement from the accident," she said. "At least, not in my favor."

"Why the devil not?"

She closed her eyes, as if that might make the facts more palatable. It didn't. It never had. "My father was at fault. He was speeding and he was drunk. Sadly he and my mother weren't the only victims. Four other people died as a result of his actions, and two more were left with crippling injuries. Because of the ensuing lawsuits, I was left with nothing but my mother's personal effects and a small insurance policy she'd taken out when I was born. And you already know how that was spent."

"They had nothing else of value? No stock portfolio or real estate?"

She shook her head. "We never owned a house, or even an apartment. Home was a top floor suite in a posh residential hotel overlooking English Bay in Vancouver. A place where they could entertain their socialite friends and host glamorous parties."

Niko muttered under his breath and she didn't have to understand Greek to know he swore. "So they could afford that, but never thought to provide for their only child's future?"

"They lived for the moment. Every day was an adventure, and money was meant to be spent. And why not? My father was hugely successful in the stock market."

"A pity he wasn't as committed to setting some aside for his daughter's future as he was to spending it on himself."

"He and my mother adored me," she flared. "They made me feel treasured and wanted. I led a charmed life, filled with warmth and laughter and love. You can't put a price on that."

"They were spoiled children playing at being adults," he countered harshly. "Even if they'd left you a fortune, it could never make up for what their fecklessness ended up costing you."

"Stop it!" she cried, not sure what angered her more: that he dared to criticize her family, or that he was right. "Just shut up!"

Throwing off the blanket, she climbed onto the side

deck and went to stand at the bow of the boat. It was the most distance she could put between them.

He came up behind her. Put his arms around her. "Hey," he said. "Listen to me."

"No. You've said enough."

"Not quite. Not until I tell you I'm sorry."

"What is it about 'shut up' that you don't understand? I'm not interested in your apology."

"And I'm not very good at taking orders. Also, I'm the last person qualified to comment on flawed relationships." He nuzzled the side of her neck, his jaw scraping lightly, erotically against her skin. "Forgive me?"

She wanted to refuse. To end things with him while she still could, and save herself more heartache down the road. Because that annoying voice of caution was whispering in her head again, warning her that this was just another in a long list of differences. They disagreed on too many critical issues ever to remain in harmony for very long. He didn't care about family. Didn't believe in love. Wasn't interested in marriage or commitment.

But the starch of her resistance was softening, leaving her body pliant to his touch, her heart susceptible to his seduction. A lot of men said the same things he had—until the right woman came along and changed their minds. Why couldn't she be the one to change his?

"Emily? Please say something. I know I've made you angry, hurt you, but please don't shut me out."

"Yes, I'm angry," she admitted miserably, "because you had no right trying to strip me of my illusions. And I'm hurt, because you succeeded." She spun around, dazzled by tears. "I've spent the last eighteen years wilfully ignoring the truth about the parents I so badly wanted to preserve as perfect in my memory. Thanks to you, I won't be able to do that anymore."

He swore again, so softly it turned into an endearment, and buried her face at his shoulder. She started to cry in earnest then, for lost dreams and fate's cruel indifference to human pain.

"Let me make it better, angel," Niko murmured, stringing kisses over her hair. "Let me love you as you deserve to be loved."

And because she wanted him more than she wanted to stay safe, she lifted her tearstained face to his and surrendered. "Yes," she said.

CHAPTER SEVEN

THE lover's grand romantic gesture—sweeping her into his arms and carrying her to bed—didn't work on a sailboat. Slender though she was, the companionway just wasn't big enough for them both at the same time. The best he could do was precede her into the main cabin and guide her as she backed down the four steps leading below deck.

Not exactly a hardship, he decided, steadying her with a hand on either side of her hips as she descended. She wasn't very tall, a little over one and a half meters, and weighed no more than about forty-six kilos, but as her slim, elegant legs crossed his line of vision, the prospect of laying them bare to his renewed inspection left him hard and aching.

Unfortunately, by the time he'd led her into the aft sleeping quarters, her eyes were enormous in her pale face, she was trembling and hyperventilating. Some men might have interpreted that as an eagerness that matched their own, but he'd seen too many refugees huddled in war zones with bombs exploding around them, to be so easily taken in.

Virgin or not, and for all that she'd seemed willing

enough when he'd asked her to let him make love to her, now that the moment lay at hand, she was afraid. And in his book, that meant ignoring the raging demands of his libido, because the day had yet to dawn that he satisfied his own needs at the expense of a woman's.

Instead he flicked on the wall lamps, and slipped a CD into the built-in sound system. With the soothing sound of a Chopin nocturne filling the silence, he drew her down to sit beside him on the edge of the bed and wiped away the remains of her tears. "You are so incredibly beautiful," he told her.

She managed a shaky laugh. "I doubt it. I never learned to cry daintily. But thank you for saying so. Most men hate it when a woman resorts to tears."

"I'm not most men," he said, running his fingers idly through her hair. It reminded him of cool satin. So did her skin when, grazing his knuckles along her jaw to her throat, he extended his slow exploration. "And you very definitely are not most women."

He touched her mouth next, teasing her lips with his thumb. Not until they parted of their own volition did he lean forward and kiss them softly.

Her eyes fell shut as if the weight of her lashes was too much to bear. She sighed. And when she did, all her pent-up tension escaped, leaving her flexible as a willow against him.

Still he did not try to rush her, but cupped his hand around her nape and touched his mouth to hers again. She tasted of wine and innocence, and only when the subtle flavor of desire entered the mix did he deepen the kiss.

Gradually she grew bolder. Her hands crept under his sweater and up his bare chest, deft and sure. She murmured, little inarticulate pleadings that said the fear was gone and she was ready. More than ready. Her hunger matched his.

Suppressing the urgency threatening his control, he undressed her at leisure, discarding her shoes and socks first, then her jogging suit. A practical outfit and attractive enough in its way, it did not merit lingering attention. But underneath, she wore peach-colored lace; a bra so delicate and fine, her nipples glowed pink through the fabric, and panties so minuscule they defied gravity.

Clinging provocatively to her body, they were so blatantly designed to stir a man to passion that he had to turn away from the sight before he embarrassed himself. Had to rip down the zippered fly of his jeans or suffer permanent injury from their confinement. Kicking them off, he yanked his sweater over his head, flung it across the cabin, and sent his briefs sailing after it.

Misunderstanding his abrupt change of pace, she stroked a tentative hand down his back and whispered, "Are you angry? Did I do something wrong?"

"You're the nurse here," he ground out roughly, spinning around so that there was no way she could miss the state he was in. "Does it look to you as if you did something wrong?"

She blinked. And blushed.

If he hadn't been such a seething mass of sexual hunger that the functioning part of his brain was concerned only with how soon he could satisfy it, he'd have told her how her shy modesty charmed him. But his stamina was nearing its limits and wanting his dwindling endurance to be focused on bringing her pleasure, he drew back the bedcovers and pulled her down to lie next to him.

Willing his obdurate flesh to patience, he undid the clasp of her bra. Slid the outrageous panties down her legs. And when at last she lay naked before him, feasted his eyes on her. Dazzled by her blond perfection, her delicate symmetry of form, and perhaps most of all by the sultry heat in her eyes, he shaped her every curve and hollow with his hands, and followed them with his mouth.

She undulated on the mattress, offering herself to him without reserve. Clutching his shoulders in swift bursts of tactile delight when he found her most sensitive spots. Arching, taut as a high-tension wire, as he brought her to the brink of orgasm. And collapsing in a puddle of heat as she surrendered to it.

That she was so responsive to his seduction gratified him, but it inflamed him, as well. He wasn't made of stone, and knew he couldn't go on indefinitely denying himself the same pleasure he afforded her.

She knew it, too, and reaching down, she closed her hand around him. With another of her engaging little sighs, she traced her fingers over his erection, glorying in its strength, cherishing its vulnerability. Did so with such reverence that she somehow managed to touch him elsewhere, in places he kept separate from other people. In his heart, in his soul.

The emotional onslaught, as singular as it was powerful, blinded him to the encroaching danger. Responsibility, finesse, all the vital prerequisites by which he defined his sexual liaisons, deserted him. He was consumed with the overwhelming need to possess and be possessed. Seeming to sense the latter, she angled her body closer and cradled him snugly between her smooth, beautiful thighs.

Her daring lured him past all caution. The blood pulsed through his loins. He could feel her damp warmth beckoning him, knew of his own near-capitulation, and with only nanoseconds to spare, he dragged himself back from the brink of insanity and sheathed himself in a condom. Then and only then did he bury himself fully within her.

Tilting her hips, she rose up to meet him, caught in his relentless rhythm, absorbing his every urgent thrust. She was sleek, hot, tight. Irresistible. She took his body hostage. Held him fast within her and rendered him mindless to everything but the rampant, inexorable surge of passion rising to a climax that threatened to destroy him.

It caught her in its fury, too. He felt her contract around him. Was dimly conscious of her muffled cries, her nails raking down his back, and then the tide crashed over him. Stripped him of power and tumbled him into helpless submission. With a groan dragged up from the depths of his soul, he flooded free.

Spent, but aware he must be crushing her with his weight, he fought to regain his breath, to regulate his racing heart. Finally, with a mighty effort, he rolled onto his side and took her with him. Glancing down, he found her watching him, her eyes soft, her lovely face flushed. A world removed from the trembling creature she'd been half an hour before.

Curious as to the reason, he said, "You were nervous when I first brought you down here, weren't you?"

"I still am."

It wasn't the answer he expected, but remembering her comment about her previous experience, he thought he knew what prompted it. "If you're thinking you disappointed me as a partner, *karthula*, be assured I could not ask for better."

"It's not that at all," she said. "Before we made love, I was afraid I'd end up liking you too much. Now I'm afraid because I know I was right."

Her admission splintered his heart a little, as if she'd driven a needle into it and caused a tiny wound. He was not accustomed to such quiet honesty from his partners. "Is that such a bad thing?" he asked her.

"Not necessarily bad. I knew making love with you meant taking a risk. I just didn't realize how big a risk."

Then don't think of it as making love, he wanted to tell her. Be like the other women I take to bed, and see it as enjoyable sex. But she was so aglow that he couldn't bring himself to disillusion her. Which, in itself, gave rise to another troubling stab to his hitherto impregnable heart. She brought out a protective tenderness in him that he found as frightening as it was unacceptable.

Reading his thoughts with daunting insight, she said, "Don't worry, Niko. I'm not so naive that I think this weekend is the prelude to a long-term relationship. I'm not expecting it to end with a proposal of marriage or a ring."

Why not?

The question so nearly escaped him that he had to bite his tongue to contain it. "I'm in no position to offer either, even if I wanted to," he said, when he recovered himself. "My career doesn't lend itself to that sort of commitment, and I doubt there are many women who'd put up with a husband who's away more often than he's at home."

"Exactly. Realistically, neither of us is in the market

for anything but a casual fling. I'm just not very good at 'casual.'"

"There's nothing wrong with liking the person you're in bed with, Emily, and if I haven't already made it clear, let me say now that I like you very much. I wouldn't have asked you to come away with me if I didn't."

Her smile turned into a thinly disguised yawn. "That's good," she said. "I'll sleep much better knowing that, but I need to brush my teeth first."

"Of course. I'll use the head—bathroom in nautical terms, in case you're wondering—in the forward cabin."

She slithered off the bed and disappeared, a too-fleeting vision of slender, lamplit femininity that stirred him to fresh arousal. But he had his own rituals to attend to, not the least of which was making sure the anchor was well set for the night. Nothing like having a sailboat run aground to ruin the romantic ambience.

When he rejoined her in the bed some fifteen minutes later, she lay on her side facing away from him and was sound asleep. Just as well, really. She made it too easy for him to forget the rules he'd long ago set for himself. To those he rescued—the orphans, the widows, the elderly—he gave everything of himself because they didn't trespass into his personal life. Those he associated with the rest of the time he'd learned to keep at a safe distance.

Even though he wasn't touching her, he lay close enough that the heat of his body coiled around her. She knew that if she turned, if she made the slightest overture, he'd take her in his arms and they'd make love again. And she couldn't do it. She was too terrified of his power over her. Terrified that as the pleasure he gave her built to an unbearable peak, she might utter the three words guaranteed to put an end to what she had rightly termed a fling.

He might like her very much, but that was light years removed from his wanting to hear her say "I love you." Not that she did love him. In fact, she knew very well that she did not. *Could* not. Because anyone with half a brain knew that blissful, incredible sex didn't equal love.

Men have a one-track mind, she once overheard an embittered nursing colleague say. *They want a woman between the sheets, and they achieve it by making you feel as if they don't want to be anywhere else but with you—until the next day or the next week, when they move on to someone else, and you're left feeling slightly shopworn and incredibly stupid. The only way to gain the upper hand is either to fool them into thinking you don't care if you never see them again, or else swear off sex altogether.*

Apart from her one dismal experience with the third-year medical resident whose ego had surpassed anything else he had to offer, Emily had subscribed to the latter. She would not risk her self-respect or her reputation for the sake of a tawdry one-night stand. What was best, she'd decided in what she now recognized as pathetic naiveté on her part, was to settle for nothing less than complete commitment before leaping into intimacy with a man. But that prudent argument was before Niko Leonidas swept into her life, and swept out all her preconceived notions of what was best.

Sharing the same bed with him now, and so graphically conscious of him that her skin vibrated with awareness, she forced herself to remain completely still as she waited for his breathing to settle into the deep, even rhythm that signaled sleep.

Seconds passed. Spun into long, painful minutes. Nothing broke the silence but the whisper of the sea and the equally subdued sound of his breathing. He was a very quiet sleeper, unlike his father who snored lustily when he nodded off.

Cautiously she shifted her foot; tucked her hand beneath her pillow. And waited for a sign that he was as wide-awake as she was. He did not stir. Convinced it was now safe to do so, she stopped pretending, opened her eyes and admitted to the moon-splashed night the awful truth.

She *was* in love with him. She had been for days. She'd committed the ultimate folly and laid on the line everything she had to give, in exchange for what she'd always known could never be more than a passing affair. And now she was paying the price.

The painful enormity of what she'd allowed to happen overwhelmed her. Tears seeped onto her pillow and silent sobs shook her body. All at once she was a child again, left with a heart full of love and no one to give it to. She wanted Niko to look at her as her father used to look at her mother, as if she was the most beautiful, fascinating creature ever to grace the earth. She wanted the magic and passion and permanence they'd known. She wanted it all, and she wanted it with Niko.

In short, she wanted what he couldn't give her.

"Emily?" His voice swam softly out of the gloom. "Are you asleep?"

"No," she muttered thickly, "but I thought you were."

She heard the rustle of the bed linen, felt his hand glide over her silky nightgown and come to rest at her hip. "Anything but," he said, his voice sinking to a husky growl. "I'm lying here thinking about you…and wanting you again."

He inched the hem of her gown up past her knees. Past her waist. His hand ventured, warm and possessive, between her thighs. "Emily?" he said again.

Any woman with an ounce of self-preservation to her name would have slapped his hand away, but not Emily Anne Tyler. No, she melted at his touch. Rolled onto her back, let her legs fall slackly apart and advertised the fact that she was more than willing to accommodate him. Well, why not, some distant part of her brain rationalized. At this point, she had nothing left to lose and might as well hoard as many precious memories as possible of this brief enchanted interlude.

He kissed the side of her neck. Murmured in her ear all the words men were supposed to murmur to a woman they planned to seduce. Words calculated to break down her resistance, to make her compliant to his every wish. Eventually he lowered himself on top of her and, pulling her legs up around his waist, eased himself smoothly inside her. As if, she thought, struggling to retain a grip on reality, God had designed them specifically for each other.

He loved her slowly this time, transporting her in leisurely increments of sensual delight until she could hold back no longer, then supporting himself on his forearms to watch her as she climaxed. When he came, she watched him, too. Saw the grim line of his mouth as he fought a battle he hadn't a hope of winning. Saw how, at the last moment, he closed his eyes and groaned as his body shuddered in helpless surrender. The unguarded honesty of it all made her cry again.

"What is it?" he asked, clearly appalled. "Did I hurt you? Tell me, *mana mou*."

"No," she said, because confessing the truth—that with every touch, every word, every glance, he made her love him all the more—wasn't an option. "Making love again was so beautiful, that's all."

A weak excuse, but thankfully he accepted it. Cradling her so that her head rested on his shoulder and his arm kept her close, he said, "It was magnificent. It will be the next time, too."

She was able to fall asleep on that promise, comforted by the steady beat of his heart beneath her hand and lulled by the gentle rise and fall of the sea beneath the boat.

They didn't wake up until almost nine o'clock. After a simple breakfast of yogurt and fruit, they took their coffee up on deck. Although summer's intense heat was long past, it was still a shorts-and-tank-top kind of day.

"By noon," he told Emily, pulling her into the curve of his arm, "you'll be lying on the foredeck, stripped down to your bikini."

"Mmm." She lifted her face to the sun. "Lolling in a bikini on a sailboat in October. Not too tough to take, I have to admit."

"Happy you decided to come away with me?"

"Who wouldn't be? It's lovely here."

Right answer, but it didn't quite ring true. Something was bothering her. "Are you sure?"

"Of course," she said, and promptly changed the

subject. "Will the water be too cold for swimming, do you think?"

"We can find out later, if you like, but it's a bit too early yet. Emily, is there something—?"

"Early! Heavens, Niko, it's after ten already. Do you always sleep in so late?"

"Only when I'm away on the boat. It's my one, sure outlet of escape from the everyday routine." He didn't add that the constant danger inherent in his work, the risks involved, took a toll. He left that part of his life behind the second he cast off from the yacht club and took to the sea.

"Burn-out, you mean? I know what that's like. It's one reason I agreed to come to Greece and nurse Pavlos back to health. I needed a change of scene."

"And the other reason?"

She chewed her lip thoughtfully. "I'd grown very fond of him during the time he was hospitalized. In a way, we'd become more like father and daughter than nurse and patient, and I didn't feel I could abandon him."

"More like grandfather and granddaughter, surely?"

"When you don't have any other family, you don't quibble about little things like that."

A month ago, he'd have taken that remark and found any number of hidden messages in it. Now, he took it at face value.

"Even after all these years, you still miss your parents, don't you?"

"Yes. Very much."

"And I made it worse with my comments last night," he muttered, cursing himself. "I tarnished your perfect memories of them."

"Not really, because nobody's perfect, not even my parents, for all that I tried so hard to idealize them. The truth is, I've sometimes thought it was as well they died young and together. They wouldn't have dealt well with old age or being alone. And I would never have filled the emptiness left behind if only one of them had been killed in the accident."

She captivated him with her honesty, which was pretty ironic considering his first impression of her had been that she wasn't to be trusted. "They might not have been perfect, Emily, but they came close to it when they made you. I'm sure they loved you very much."

"Oh, they loved me," she said, moving away from him and gazing mistily at the blue horizon, "but they never really needed me. If you must know, that's why I decided to become a nurse. I wanted to be needed. You don't, though, do you?"

Her question threw him. "Why else do you think I put my life on the line to help other people?"

"Because they're strangers who invade your professional life for just a little while. But your personal life…well, that's different. It's off-limits. A person only has to look at your relationship with your father, to see that."

She saw too much, and he wouldn't sink so low as to deny it. "Having him join the party isn't my idea of a good time, Emily."

She made a face. "My fault. I'm the one who mentioned him."

"Then I suggest we make a concerted effort to get rid of him. What do you say we take the dinghy ashore and go for a walk on the island?"

"I'd love to," she said with alacrity. "Let me get my camera."

Her relief was palpable. Because she didn't want his father hanging around, either, Niko wondered, or because she wanted to put distance between the two of them?

He shouldn't have cared, one way or the other. Annoyingly he did.

CHAPTER EIGHT

A GREAT suggestion, Emily concluded, watching as Niko tilted the outboard engine clear of the water and the bottom of the dinghy scraped onto the narrow strip of gravelly beach edging the island. Luxuriously comfortable though it might be, the yacht's big drawback was that it offered no means of escape when the conversation got out of hand. And it had, dangerously so, straying close to disastrous when she foolishly brought up the business of wanting to be needed. Another few minutes and her feelings for Niko, which she was so desperately trying to suppress, would have spilled out.

Hiding behind her camera gave her the chance to regroup. She took pictures of flowers enjoying a riotous last bloom before winter: wild geraniums and gaudy poppies; daisies and ice plant in shades of mauve and white. She snapped the yacht riding peacefully at anchor in the sheltered bay. And when he least expected it, she captured images of Niko; of his dazzling smile, his chiseled profile, his lashes lowered to half-mast as he squinted against the brightness of the sparkling sea.

The atmosphere on the island was different, she realized. Freer, less soberly intense. Here, she could breathe and not have to worry about keeping up her guard. If necessary, she could put distance between her and Niko. Contrarily, because she could, she felt no need to do so.

Sensing her change of mood, he matched it with a lighthearted teasing of his own. "If you didn't have a camera slung around your wrist, you'd be up to your neck in trouble," he growled with mock ferocity, grabbing her before she could escape after she'd caught him unaware at the water's edge and splashed him.

That kind of trouble she could handle. "I wish I could say I'm sorry, and mean it," she returned cheekily, and splashed him again.

Suddenly his laughter faded and twining her hands in his, he regarded her searchingly. "*I* wish I could take you away for a month, instead of a weekend," he said. "Being around you is good for me, Emily. You remind me that there's more to living than burying myself in work. I'm a happy man when I'm with you."

Her spirit soared at that. Could he possibly be falling for her, too?

Well, why not? Wasn't she forever telling her patients and their families that they should never give up hope? And hadn't she seen for herself, time and time again, that miracles did happen? Why couldn't one come her way for a change?

"Keep looking at me like that," he went on, his voice lowering to a thrilling purr, "and I won't be held liable for what I might do, which would be a mistake on two counts. This beach isn't designed for comfortable seduction, and even if it were, I didn't bring a contraceptive with me."

Flirting shamelessly, she glanced up at him in her

best imitation of a siren bent on luring him to destruction. "Then why don't we go back to the yacht?"

His eyes darkened, turned a deep forest-green. "Race you to the dinghy, angel."

Love in the afternoon was different, she discovered. Sunlight pouring through the window above the bed and casting dancing reflections of the sea on the cabin ceiling brought an openness to intimacy that, at first, dismayed her because it left her with no place to hide.

He soon put paid to that nonsense. He examined her all over, from the soles of her feet to the top of her head. He found the tiny scar on her bottom where she'd fallen on broken glass at the beach when she was little, and he kissed it as if it were new and still hurting.

He paid attention to every inch of her, sometimes with his hands, sometimes with his mouth and tongue, pausing every now and then to murmur, "Do you like it when I do this?"

Like? She'd never before felt such slow, rolling awareness of herself as a woman. He made her quiver with anticipation. He brought her body to electrifying life and made it yearn and ache and throb. He made her scream softly and beg for more.

Until him, she'd never climaxed. With him, she came so quickly and with such fury that she couldn't catch her breath.

His touch sent her flying so high, she could almost touch the heavens, and he knew it because he watched her the entire time. Knew to the second when she hovered on the brink, and tipped her over the edge into a glorious, sparkling free-fall she wished might never end.

Then, when she was dazed with exhausted pleasure and sure she didn't have the strength to lift a finger, let alone peak again, he buried himself in her hot, sleek folds and taught her otherwise. Caught in his urgent, driving rhythm, she swooped and soared with him again to a magnificent crashing finale.

At two in the afternoon or thereabouts, they put together a snack of fruit and cheese and ate it in the shade of the canvas bimini in the cockpit. They drank a little wine, and they talked, mostly about Niko as it turned out, which inevitably meant Pavlos crept back into the conversation, too.

"Was he cruel to you?" Emily asked, when Niko spoke briefly of his unhappy childhood.

"Not in the way you're thinking," he said. "Far from it. I never lacked for a thing. Clothes, toys, tutors, whatever I needed, he provided. When it came to my later education, there was no limit to how far he'd go to make sure I had the best. He sent me to the most prestigious boarding school in Europe—more than one in fact, since I managed to get myself kicked out of several."

"Then why the estrangement?"

"He didn't understand that there was more to being a father than spending money."

"Or else he didn't understand that you were crying out for his love."

"It was never about love with him. It was about power. And from his point of view, money and power are one and the same. Which is another bone of contention between us because to me, money's merely the means to an end. If I end up without any, I'll find a way to make more, but I'll never let it rule my life the way it rules his."

"Why do you think he sets such store by it?"

"Probably because he grew up without any. He was the by-product of an affair between a housemaid and the son of her millionaire employer who abandoned her when he learned she was pregnant. If you asked him what his most driving ambition had been when he was a boy, I guarantee he'd say it was to end up one of the wealthiest men in Greece, able to pick and choose his friends, his associates and, eventually, his wife."

"He appears to have succeeded."

Niko inclined his head in agreement. "Yes, but it took him years. He didn't marry my mother until he was thirty-one which, back then, was considered pretty old. She was just twenty, and the only daughter of one of his biggest business rivals."

"Is that why he married her—to score points over her father?"

"No," he said. "He really loved her. I have to give him credit for that much."

"What a shame he could never see you as her most lasting legacy to him."

"I was too much the rebel, refusing to toe the Leonidas line, determined to go my own way and to hell with anyone who tried to stop me."

He'd never been so open with her before. Was it the lazy afternoon heat or their lovemaking that made it easier for him to share his life story with her now? Whatever the reason, Emily was hungry to know everything about him and prepared to listen for as long as he was willing to talk. "Did he want you to go to university?"

"In the worst way, and was pretty convinced he could make it happen since I wouldn't have any money of my own until I turned twenty-one. He saw a business degree as the next logical step to my joining his empire. But I got out from under his control when I joined the air force, and there wasn't a damned thing he could do about it. After I left the service, I spent a year in England with a former UN pilot who taught me everything he knew about mercy missions, and introduced me to the finer points of the English language. After that, I came back to Greece, took over my inheritance and set up my own operation."

"And the rest, as they say, is history?"

He stood up and stretched. "*Ne*—and pretty dull at that, if you ask me, not to mention a criminal waste of a beautiful afternoon. What do you say to a swim?"

He was finished baring his soul and, for now at least, she realized she'd gain nothing by pressing for more. "Okay, if you're sure the water's warm enough."

"Only one way to find out, Emily," he said, dragging her to her feet. "You coming in of your own free will, or do I throw you in?"

"At least let me change into my bikini."

"What for?" He dropped his shorts and briefs, pulled off his T-shirt and climbed onto the swim grid in all his beautiful naked glory. "Nothing like going au naturel, as they say in polite society, especially as neither of us has anything to show that the other hasn't already seen."

"Once a rebel, always a rebel," she muttered self-consciously as she peeled off her clothes.

He favored her with a lascivious grin. "I hardly expected a nurse to be so modest, my dear. Even your bottom's blushing."

There was only one response to that remark and she

wasted no time delivering it. Bracing both hands against his chest, she shoved him into the water. He landed with a mighty splash and she followed suit before he had the chance to climb back on board and exact his revenge.

After the first chilling shock, the sea was deliciously refreshing. Heaven had never seemed so close, Emily decided, floating on her back with her hair streaming out behind her and the big blue bowl of the sky arcing overhead.

Niko, whom she'd last seen swimming in a powerful crawl toward the mouth of the bay, suddenly bobbed to the surface next to her. "You look like a mermaid," he said. "A particularly delectable mermaid."

And he looked like a sea god, she thought, her heart turning over at the sight of his broad, tanned shoulders, his brilliant smile and the thick lashes spiking in clumps around his remarkable green eyes. Small wonder she'd fallen in love with him. What woman in her right mind could resist him?

They climbed back on board and lay down on the foredeck to dry in the sun's benign warmth. He'd swum farther than he intended, a strenuous workout that left him pleasantly tired and happy just to lie next to her, his limbs touching hers, his fingers brushing lightly against her arm. Not moving, not speaking, just looking into her dark blue eyes and letting utter contentment sweep over him.

Was he falling in love?

He couldn't be. It was completely out of the question. A misguided romantic fantasy brought on by brain fatigue or some other disorder of the mind, because he absolutely refused to entertain the possibility that it might have something to do with his heart. Yet if it was so impossible, why did he suddenly hate the man who'd taken her virginity? She belonged to no one but him, and should have waited until he found her.

"What dark thoughts are chasing through your mind?" she murmured drowsily, peering at him from half-closed eyes.

The unpalatable truth rose in his throat, bitter as bile. Scowling, he said, "I have a confession to make. More than one, in fact."

"Oh?" A shadow flitted over her face. "Such as?"

"For a start, I'm jealous of my predecessor."

Clearly at a loss, she said, "What are you talking about?"

"I'm jealous of whoever it was that you slept with before you met me."

"I see." She pushed herself up on one elbow, propped her head on her hand and regarded him thoughtfully. "Should I be flattered?"

"I don't know. I've never found myself in this kind of situation before."

And that, he thought, was the whole problem in a nutshell.

Before he met her, sex had been all about mutual pleasure with no strings attached. He never lied to his willing partners, never made promises he couldn't keep, was never intentionally cruel. But sometimes he hurt them anyway because they wanted more than he could give.

Until now. Until Emily, when his initial plan had somehow gone terribly wrong and he found himself in danger of wanting to give much more than he could ever afford.

"That doesn't sit well with you, does it?" she said.

"No. I prefer to stick to the rules."

"What rules?"

"Those I've set for myself."

"And you're breaking them with me?"

"Yes," he said grimly, uncertain whether it was self-preservation or self-destruction that drove him to bare his soul so brutally. "When I first started seeing you, all I ever intended was to act as a decoy."

"A decoy?"

He heard the wariness in her voice edging closer to outright dismay, and wished he'd kept his mouth shut. But palming her off with half-truths left him feeling dirty and unworthy of her. And even if it didn't, he'd said too much to stop now. "Yes," he said. "To keep you away from my father. There being no fool like an old fool, I decided to step in and save him from himself— and you—by diverting your attention from an ailing old man to one who could better please you."

Dazed, she glanced away and focused her attention on the boat, appearing fascinated by its sleek lines, gleaming fiberglass deck and oiled teak. "So this weekend is all about proving a point?"

"No. That's the trouble. Now it's about you and me, and feelings I never bargained for. I tried to tell you this the other night, but I lost my nerve."

She wasn't listening. Instead she was scrambling to her feet and swinging her head wildly from side to side, a wounded creature desperate to escape her tormentor.

Springing to her side, he trapped her in his arms. She

lashed out at him, catching him a glancing blow on the jaw. "Let me go!" she spat. "Don't ever touch me again!"

"You're not hearing me, Emily," he told her urgently. "Everything's different now."

"Sure it is." She was sobbing. The sound drove splinters through his heart. "You've finally shown your true colors."

"No, Emily. I made a stupid mistake."

"So you decided to make it up to me by giving me a weekend to remember? How tedious you must have found it, pretending you wanted to have sex with me."

"I wasn't pretending! For God's sake, Emily, you of all people know a man can't pretend."

"So how did you manage? By closing your eyes and imagining I was someone else?"

He crushed her to him, shocked. "Never. It was always you. Only you, right from the start. I just didn't realize it at the time."

"And here I thought we'd put to rest that whole ludicrous notion that I was some sort of fortune hunter out to fleece your poor father." She wasn't crying now. She was encased in ice.

"We have," he protested. "You are what you've always been, as beautiful on the inside as you are on the surface."

"I don't feel beautiful," she said tonelessly. "I feel stupid and pathetic, because I let myself fall in love with you."

"Then I guess we're both stupid and pathetic, because that's what I'm trying to say. I'm falling in love with you, too, and the damnable thing is, I don't know what the hell to do about it."

"Then I'll tell you," she said. "You get over it. We both do."

* * *

The look on his face told her it wasn't the answer he wanted to hear. "Why should we?" he whispered against her mouth.

But the damage was done and nothing he said or did could put things right again. "Because there's no future in it for either of us." She pulled away just far enough to look him in the eye, then added pointedly, "Is there?"

"If you're asking me to predict what might happen tomorrow, I can't, Emily. All any of us ever has is today. Can't you let that be enough?"

Temporary bliss, in exchange for long-term misery? Not a chance! She was in enough pain already, and prolonging the inevitable would merely increase the agony. "No. I made up my mind long before I met you that relationships heading nowhere are a waste of time."

"I could change your mind, if you'd let me."

She was terribly afraid that he could, and knew she had to get away from him before he succeeded. He was kissing her eyes, her hair, her throat. Stroking his hands down her arms and up her bare back with killing tenderness. Sabotaging her with caresses when words failed to get him what he wanted, and already her resistance was dissolving under the attack.

"I don't want to be here with you anymore," she said, clinging to her vanishing resolve with the desperation of a drowning woman. "Take me back to the mainland."

"I will," he murmured. "Tomorrow."

"Tonight."

"*Ohi*...no." He lifted her off her feet and set her down in the cockpit. Traced his lips over her cheek and brought his mouth to hers and kissed her softly.

He made her legs shake, her insides quiver. He made her heart yearn. "Please," she whimpered helplessly.

"Give me one last night, my Emily."

"I can't."

He touched her fleetingly between the legs. "Tell me why not, when I know you want me as much as I want you."

She shuddered, caught in the clenching grip of rising passion. "Tell me why I'm inexplicably drawn to a man who isn't at all my kind of man," she countered.

"And what kind of man is that?"

"The kind who's not afraid of love. Who's happy with a nine-to-five job and a mortgage," she said, grasping at a truth she'd refused to acknowledge until now. "The safe kind who doesn't need to flirt with danger all the time in order to find fulfillment."

"Then you're right. I'm definitely not your kind of man."

But he pulled her closer, and the way her body tilted to meet his, welcoming the questing nudge of his erection, proclaimed otherwise. As if she'd finally found what she'd always been looking for. As if he was exactly her kind of man.

She was lost, and she knew it. The irrepressible pulse of his flesh against hers enthralled her. Lured her into forgetting how he had deceived and used her. Nothing mattered except to know again the pleasure only he could give. If, the next day or the next week, he reneged on his protestations of love, at least she'd have this weekend to remember him by.

The hunger, rapacious, insatiable, spiraled to unbearable heights. Casting aside all pretense at dignity, she sprawled on the cockpit cushions. At once, he was on top of her. Thrusting inside her, hot, heavy, demanding.

Perfectly attuned, they rose and sank together, pausing at just the right moment to drown in each other's gaze. There was no need for words to justify a decision that went against everything they'd just said to each other. They had come together because they could not stay apart. It was as simple as that.

CHAPTER NINE

WHEN they finally stirred and she mentioned that she'd like to freshen up, Niko ran a critical hand over his jaw, said he could use a shower and shave himself and told her not to rush. "We have all the time in the world," he said. "We'll have mezedes and wine and watch the moon rise, then eat dinner when the mood takes us."

So she indulged herself in a leisurely bath, and shampooed the saltwater out of her hair. After toweling herself dry, she massaged lotion into her sun-kissed skin, spritzed a little cologne at her elbows and behind her knees and put on the silk caftan, glad she'd had the good sense to smuggle it aboard. He'd said he was in love with her, but she sensed he'd made the admission reluctantly, and pinned little hope on his feeling the same way in the morning. If so, and if this turned out to be their last night together, she intended it to be one neither of them would soon forget.

Nor did they, but not for the reasons she'd supposed. The very second she joined him in the main cabin, she knew their plans had changed. He'd showered—his damp hair attested to that—but he hadn't shaved. There was no sign of the appetizers he'd mentioned, no tempting aromas drifting from the oven, no wine chilling. All that lay on the table was his cell phone, and one look at his face told her it had been the bearer of bad news. "Something's happened," she said, a sinking feeling in the pit of her stomach.

"Yes. I'm afraid we have to head back right away."

"Is it Pavlos?"

He shook his head. "I just got word from my director of operations that we've lost contact with one of our pilots in north Africa. He was scheduled to pick up an injured Red Cross worker from a refugee camp. He never showed up."

"What can you do about it?"

He stared at her as if she wasn't in command of all her faculties. "Go find him. What did you think—that I'd sit back and leave him stranded in the desert?"

"No, of course not." She swallowed, stung by his brusque tone. "Is there any way that I can help?"

"Change into something warmer, for a start. That thing you've got on won't do. Quite a stiff onshore breeze has sprung up. It'll be a chilly trip back to the mainland."

She must have looked as forlorn as she felt because when he spoke again, his voice softened. "I know you're disappointed, Emily. I am, too. This isn't how I'd foreseen the evening playing out. But when situations like this come up, I'm afraid everything else has to go on hold. A man's life could be at stake."

"I understand," she said. And she did. Completely. But what about *his* life? How safe would he be, rushing off to the rescue without knowing the danger he might be facing? "Will it be risky, your going looking for him?"

"It's possible, but so what? Risks come with the job. You get used to it."

You, maybe, but not me, she thought, the harsh reality of his vocation hitting home with a vengeance for the first time and filling her with apprehension. "How will you know where to start looking for him?"

"If he's turned on his epurb—electronic positioning beacon, that is—it'll lead me straight to him. If not, I'm familiar with the area, I know where he was headed and his coordinates before he lost contact."

"What if you still don't find him?"

"That's not an option," he said flatly. "He's just a kid of twenty-three, the eldest of four children and the only son of a widow. It's my job to locate him and bring him home to his family. They need him."

"But what if—?"

He silenced her with a swift, hard kiss. "No 'what ifs.' It's not the first time I've had to do this, and it won't be the last. I'll be back before you know it—by tomorrow night at the latest, but we really need to get going now if I'm to be ready to set out at first light in the morning."

Set out to where? Some vast arid region miles from civilization? Some rebel stronghold where human life didn't count for a thing? "Then I'd better get organized," she said, and turned away before he saw the desolation in her eyes.

"At least my father will be glad to have you back earlier than expected."

"I suppose."

He came up behind her and wound his arms around

her waist. "Did I mention how lovely you look, Emily?" he said softly against her hair.

On the outside, maybe. But inside, she was falling apart.

The nurse who'd replaced her was so happy to be relieved of her job, she practically flew out of the villa before Emily stepped in. "Is impossible!" she screeched, indignation fracturing her English almost past recognition. "He die, then *me niazi*! I do not care. One day more, I break his neck. *Adio.* Please not call me again. *Apokliete!*"

"Have a nice night," Emily said wearily, as the front door slammed shut in her face.

Pavlos didn't even pretend to hide his glee when she appeared at breakfast the next morning. "Didn't take you long to come to your senses, did it, girl?" he crowed.

"Try to behave yourself for a change, Pavlos," she snapped. "I'm in no mood for your shenanigans."

He smirked into his coffee cup. "That bad, was it? Could have told you it would be."

"For your information, I had a wonderful time. The only reason I came back early is that your son has gone searching for a young pilot lost somewhere over the Sahara."

His derision faded into something approaching concern, but he covered it quickly. "Damned fool! Serve him right if he got himself killed."

"I'll pretend I didn't hear you say that."

"Why not?" he retorted. "Ignoring the facts isn't going to change them. Wherever the latest hotbed of unrest shows up, you can bet he'll be there, and one of these days he'll push his luck too far."

Ill-timed though it might be, the truth of his answer could not be denied, and how she got through the rest of the day she didn't know. The minutes dragged, the hours lasted a small eternity. Morning became afternoon, then evening and, all too soon, night. Every time the phone rang, her heart plummeted. And sank lower still when the call brought no news of Niko.

"Better get used to this if you plan on sticking with him," Pavlos advised her, as the dinner hour came and went without any word.

"The same way you have?" she shot back. "You talk a good line, Pavlos, but you're as worried about him as I am."

"Not me," he huffed, but there was no real conviction in his tone and his gaze wandered to the clock on the wall every bit as often as hers did. "Where did you say he'd gone?"

"North Africa—the desert—I'm not sure exactly."

"Hmm." He drummed his arthritic old fingers on the edge of the table. "That's a lot of ground for one man to cover."

She closed her eyes. Fear beat a tattoo in her blood.

"Go to bed, Emily," Pavlos said with uncommon gentleness. "I'll wait up and let you know if we hear anything."

As if she could sleep! "I'm not tired. You should rest, though."

But neither made any move. Anxiety thick as molasses held them paralyzed.

Just after eleven o'clock, the phone shrieked into the silence one last time. Hands shaking, she grabbed it on the first ring. "Niko?"

She heard his smile. "Who else were you expecting at this hour?"

"No one…you…but it grew so late and you hadn't called—"

"You're going to have to learn to believe what I tell you, Emily," he said. "I promised I'd be back today, and I am."

"Yes." Giddy with relief, she reached for Pavlos's hand and squeezed it. "Where are you now?"

"At the office. I'll be heading home as soon as I've filed my report."

"And the man you went to find?"

"Had a fire in his control panel that knocked out his communications system. He made an emergency landing on a deserted Second World War airstrip. There are dozens of them, hundreds even, all over the Sahara. The one he chose lay nearly two hundred kilometers from where he was supposed to be, but his epurb was still working and led me straight to him."

"And he's okay?"

"He's fine, though I wish I could say the same for the aircraft. But the good news is, we picked up the man he was supposed to bring back and got him to a hospital, albeit twenty-four hours later than expected."

"You've put in a long day and must be exhausted."

"Nothing an early night won't fix. I'll see you tomorrow?"

"I can't wait," she said. "I missed you."

"Same here, *karthula*." His yawn echoed down the line. "I'd come over now, but—"

"Don't even think about it. Go home and catch up on your sleep."

"Will do. *Kali nikhta*, my sweet Emily."

"Kali nikhta," she replied. "Good night."

* * *

In the days following, she should have been completely happy. Although he vetoed any suggestion that he should terminate her employment, Pavlos was on the road to recovery and didn't need her as he once had. Accepting that she and his son were an item, he compromised by letting her take the weekends off.

She lived for the sheer heaven of those two days and nights. Niko's spacious penthouse in Kolonaki was their retreat. The living and dining rooms and en suite guest room opened onto a terrace. A small library and starkly modern kitchen comprised the rest of the main floor, with a gorgeous master suite upstairs. The decor was as spare and elegant as he himself, lacking any of the usual personal touches like photographs, but the huge collection of books and CDs told her much about his tastes and hinted at a man content with his own company.

He did his best to please her during their time together; to make it seem they were like any other couple in love. Working around his erratic schedule, they explored the countryside, going by scooter if the weather allowed but, with the cooler temperatures of November, more often by car.

They hiked in the pine-covered hills behind the town, took a picnic hamper and sailed down the coast of the Attic peninsula. Sometimes, they drove to out-of-the-way villages where they sampled wonderful local dishes in quaint, unpretentious tavernas whose walls were lined with wine barrels. Other times, they went into Athens and dined in fine style on the best the city had to offer. They danced cheek to cheek in the Grande Bretagne Hotel; made passionate love in his king-size bed.

If he had to break a date—and he did, often—he sent

her flowers, or texted messages to her in the night so that she found them on waking. In return, she tried to keep her anxiety under control when he was away, but never knew a moment's real peace until he returned. She couldn't sleep and walked the floor half the night. She couldn't eat because anxiety robbed her of her appetite. Noticing, Pavlos never missed the chance to tell her she was making the biggest mistake of her life.

She learned to live with all of it because the alternative—to put an end to it—was unthinkable.

Once, when Niko discovered he'd left his cell phone on his desk at work and had to go back to get it, he took her with him and showed her around the private airfield that served as his base of operations. The flat-roofed office building had only four rooms but was equipped with the latest in electronic equipment. Probably the aircraft sitting on the tarmac were, too, but when Emily first saw them, what struck her most forcibly was how flimsy they seemed.

"Are they what you use to fly overseas?" she asked, trying to mask her dismay.

Discerning it anyway, Niko laughed and said, "Were you expecting hot air balloons, my darling?"

"No, but these things are so small and…old-fashioned."

"Old-fashioned?" He regarded her in mock horror over the top of his aviator sunglasses.

"Well, yes. They've each got two sets of those spider-leg propellor things stuck on the front."

"I know," he said dryly. "They're what get them off the ground and keep them in the air."

"But why wouldn't you use jets? Surely they're faster?"

"Faster, but not nearly as versatile or fuel-efficient.

Twin-engine piston aircraft like these don't require nearly as long a runway as a jet, can land just about anywhere and fly at a much lower altitude." He eyed her mischievously. "Would you like me to take you up in one and show you what it can do?"

"No, thanks," she said hurriedly. "I'll take your word for it."

As they were leaving, they ran into Dinos Melettis, Niko's second-in-command. "Bring her to dinner," he insisted, after the introductions were made. "Come today. We have nothing on the board until later in the week, which makes it a good night to relax with friends, and Toula would love to meet the lady in your life. Toula," he added to Emily in an aside, "is my wife."

They accepted the invitation and had a delightful evening. "Never before has Niko brought a ladyfriend to our home," Toula confided to Emily in her careful English. "He is very enamored of you, I think."

The way he pressed his knee against hers under cover of the table and muttered between courses that he couldn't wait to get her alone again, Emily thought so, too. Yet for all that the passion between them burned brighter by the day, not once in all those weeks did they talk about the future. To do so would have shattered a present made forever uncertain by the demands of his job.

Although Emily did her best to live with that, what she couldn't get over, what terrified her, was the nature of the work that took him away from her, and the fact he always assigned himself to the most dangerous missions.

When she dared to ask him why, he said, "Because I have the most experience and the least to lose."

"But what about Vassili?" she pressed, referring to another colleague they'd bumped into one day at a kafenion in Athens. "You told me he's one of the most skilled pilots you've ever come across."

"He also has a wife and two-year-old son at home," Niko replied.

His answer and all it implied chilled her to the bone.

One Sunday evening in mid November, they stood on the terrace outside his penthouse, sipping cognac and admiring the night view of Athens spread out below. But even though Niko appeared perfectly relaxed and content, a shimmering tension emanated from him, one Emily now recognized all too well, and she braced herself for what she knew was coming.

He didn't leave her in suspense very long. "I'm off again tomorrow," he said, as deceptively casual as if he were planning to play golf, but then added guardedly, "I might be gone a bit longer than usual."

In other words, this undertaking was riskier than most. "How much longer?"

"Three days, possibly four, but you can count on my being home by the weekend."

"Where to this time?"

"Africa again."

A typically ambiguous reply. He never elaborated about his exact itinerary, was always deliberately vague about why he had to go. *Delivering food and clothing to an orphanage...survival kits to a village cut off by a landslide...a medivac rescue...supplies to a field hospital,* he'd say offhandedly when she questioned him, then quickly change the subject.

But she knew it was never as straightforward or simple as he made it sound. If it were, he wouldn't come back looking so drawn. He wouldn't wake up bathed in sweat from a nightmare he refused to talk about. He wouldn't reach for her in the night as if she was all that stood between him and an abyss of utter despair.

"Where in Africa?" she persisted now.

"Does it matter?"

"Yes, it matters."

He hesitated and she hung on tenterhooks, waiting for his answer. When he told her, it was so much worse than anything she'd let herself contemplate, was such a hellhole of violence, devastation and peril, that she felt sick to her stomach.

She knew how she was supposed to respond. Calmly. With acceptance. And she couldn't do it. Not this time. Instead she started to cry.

"Ah, Emily," he murmured and held her close. "Don't do this. We still have tonight."

But she'd broken the rules and commited the cardinal sin of wanting tomorrow, and tonight was no longer enough.

Her tears caught him off guard. Angry with himself for distressing her, and with her, too, because she'd known from the first the career he'd chosen for himself, he said, "This is why, until now, I've avoided serious involvement with a woman. When I take off on assignment, my attention has to focus on people whose lives, for one reason or another, are in jeopardy. Worrying about you is a distraction I neither need nor can afford."

"I know." She swiped at her tears and attempted a valiant smile. "I'm being selfish and unreasonable. Sorry. I don't know what came over me. I'm not usually so emotional."

She hadn't been during the early days of their affair, he had to admit. Lately, though, the smallest thing seemed to upset her. Just last week, he'd gone to pick her up at the villa and found her all teary-eyed over a bird that had flown into a window and broken its neck. He wasn't very happy about the poor thing's untimely end, either, but she knew every bit as well as he did that death was part of life and didn't differentiate between old and young, guilty or innocent.

"If this is harder than you thought it would be and want out," he said now, "just say so. I'll understand."

She closed her eyes against another bright gleam of tears and shook her head. "More than anything else, I want you."

"Even with all the baggage I bring with me?"

"Even then."

He wanted her, too. Enough that he'd willfully over-stepped the limitations he'd imposed on his personal life prior to knowing her. And at that moment, with her body haloed in the nimbus of light from the city, and her beautiful face upturned to his in vulnerable despair, he had never wanted her more. "Then come with me now," he whispered, drawing her inside and up the spiral stair-case to the bedroom. "Let's not waste the few hours re-maining before I have to leave you."

That night, unlike some when his desire for her overrode any attempt at finesse, he loved her at leisure. Caring only about pleasing her and driving the demons of fear from her mind, he kissed her all over. He seduced her with his hands, with his tongue. He hoarded the scent and texture of her skin. He watched the slow, hot flush of passion steal over her, tasted the honeyed warmth between her thighs. He commited to memory the tight rosy buds of her nipples and the little cry she made when she came.

When at last he entered her, he did so slowly. Wished he could remain forever locked within her tight, silken warmth. And when his body betrayed him, as it always did, he surrendered all that he was or ever wanted to be. *"S'agapo, chrisi mou kardhia,"* he groaned. "I love you, Emily."

He awoke just after dawn, left the bed quietly and in order not to disturb her, took his clothes and went to the guest bathroom to shower and prepare for the day ahead. When he was done, he returned to the master suite and stood a moment, watching her sleep.

Early sunlight caught the sweep of her eyelashes. Cast a pearly shadow along the line of her collarbone. Her hair fell in captivating disorder over the pillow. Her arm reached across to his side of the bed as if seeking him.

He wanted to touch her. Put his mouth on hers and whisper her name. And knew he could not, because doing so would make it impossible for him to leave her.

Turning away, he picked up his bag and quietly let himself out of the penthouse.

CHAPTER TEN

COMPULSIVE worry took over her life and gnawed at it until it was full of holes. Holes that tormented her every waking hour and haunted her dreams.

Niko had willingly flown into an area where none of the rules of the civilized world applied. Every day, news reports of unspeakable atrocities made the headlines. Murder, banditry and torture were commonplace; starvation and disease had reached epic proportions.

Intellectually Emily recognized that helpless men, women and children desperately needed the kind of humanitarian relief people like Niko dedicated themselves to providing. But the Geneva Convention had no meaning for the perpetrators of the crimes being committed, and those trying to help were finding themselves subjected to increasing violence, some of it so extreme they were being evacuated for their own safety. Others had lost their lives for the principles they believed in.

What if he became one of them?

Self-fulfilling prophecies were dangerous in themselves, she realized, and in an effort to divert her mind into other channels, she turned to anger. Why had he left without saying goodbye? To spare them both the pain of a farewell, or because he cared more about strangers than he did about her?

But that line of reasoning merely shamed her. How could any thinking person, let alone a woman who'd made caring for those unable to care for themselves her vocation, be so blindly selfish? His compassion for others was one of the main reasons she loved him so desperately.

She then turned to optimism, telling herself that he was the best at what he did. He'd never lost a pilot and to make sure he never did, insisted every man involved in his operation, himself included, constantly hone his skills to remain at the top of his game. "Emergencies aren't the exception," he'd once told her, "they're the rule, and we're always prepared."

How could she not support such heroic measures? How could she resent his taking a few days away from her to make a difference in the lives of those so much less fortunate? By Saturday, she'd be in his arms again and the nightmare would have passed.

But the weekend came and went with no word from him. By Monday morning she couldn't hold herself together any longer and broke down in front of Pavlos. "I'm worried sick about him," she sobbed.

"That's what happens when you get involved with a man like him."

"You make it sound as if I had a choice about falling in love with him, but that's not how it works. It happened despite my better judgment."

"What can I say? I tried to warn you, girl, but you wouldn't listen and now you're caught in a trap with no way out."

"You're not helping," she wailed, swabbing at her tears.

He looked at her sadly. "Because I can't help. I learned a long time ago that where my son is concerned, worrying's a waste of time. He's going to do what he wants to do, and to hell with anyone or anything that stands in his way."

"How do you sleep at night, Pavlos?" she cried bitterly. "How do you turn your back on your only child and not give a damn whether he lives or dies?"

"Years of practice at being unpleasant, girl. The way I see it, if I make him dislike me enough, he'll survive just to annoy me. My advice to you is the same as it's always been: forget you ever met him. You're better off not knowing what he's up to."

But she'd passed that point of no return weeks ago, and the uncertainty of not knowing was killing her. Another endless night of pacing the floor, and she'd lose her mind, so that afternoon while Pavlos napped, she took a taxi to the airfield. Better to learn the worst than be held hostage to the horrors her imagination so willingly conjured up.

The big hangar stood empty and only five aircraft waited on the tarmac, but several cars were parked outside the flat-roofed office. Not bothering to knock, she opened the door and stepped inside.

Huddled around a chart spread out on the desk in the reception area, three men and a woman talked quietly. She recognized Dinos and Toula; the other two were strangers. On hearing the door open, all four looked up and at the sight of her, their conversation subsided into a ghastly silence that fairly screamed of disaster.

"Emily." Dinos came forward with a smile. But it was a poor, pitiful effort that soon faded.

"You know something," she said, every fear she'd entertained over the last week crystalizing into certainty. "Tell me."

He didn't pretend not to understand what she was talking about. "We know nothing," he told her quietly. "We are waiting—"

"Waiting for what? To learn he's been taken captive? That he's dead?"

"There is no reason to assume either. He is a little overdue, that is all."

"Overdue?" She heard the shrill edge of hysteria climbing in her voice and could do nothing to control it. "He's *missing*, Dinos!"

At that, Toula came forward and grasped her hands. *"Ohi.* Do not distress yourself, Emily. He will return. He always does."

"How do you know that? When was the last time anyone heard from him?"

Again that awful silence descended, so thick it caused a tightness in her chest. She'd experienced the same suffocating sensation once before, the day she learned her parents had been killed.

"Thursday," Dinos finally said. "But in itself, that is not necessarily significant. Sometimes it is safer to remain incommunicado in hostile territory than risk giving away one's whereabouts."

He was lying and doing it badly. "You don't have the foggiest idea where he is or what's happened to him, do you?"

His gaze faltered and he shrugged miserably. "No."

She felt the tears pressing hot behind her eyes and fought to control them. "When were you planning to tell me? Or aren't I entitled to be kept informed?"

"Today I come to you," Toula interrupted. "That is why I am here first. To learn what is latest news and hope it will be good."

Hollow with despair, Emily said, "How do you do it, Toula? If Dinos doesn't show up when he's supposed to, how do hold on to your sanity?"

"I believe," she said, her dark eyes filled with pity. "I pray to God, and I wait. It is all I can do. It is what you must do also. You must not lose faith."

"Toula's right, Emily." Dinos touched her shoulder gently. "You must believe that whatever has happened, Niko will find his way back to you."

"*Neh*…yes." The other two men nodded vigorously.

"There is nothing you can do here," Dinos continued, guiding her to the door. "Go back to the villa and wait for him there. I will call you the very second I have anything to report. Where did you leave your car?"

"I came by taxi."

"Then Toula will drive you home."

Dinos didn't call. No one did. Instead as she was passing through the foyer late on Tuesday afternoon, she heard the sound of a vehicle departing down the driveway. A moment later, the doorbell rang. Fearing the worst, she rushed to answer and came face-to-face with Niko.

Bathed in the orange glow cast by the setting sun, he leaned against the wall, his left arm held close to his chest. "I hear you've been inquiring about me," he said.

She'd prayed for just such a miracle so often in the

last few days. Had rehearsed exactly what she'd say, what she'd do. But now that it had come to pass, she was at a loss for words and simply stared at him.

In one respect, he looked much as he had that long-ago day they'd met at the airport. Same blue jeans, open-necked shirt and black leather bomber jacket. Same rangy height, black hair and mesmerizing green eyes. But that man had been the picture of health. So strong and invincible, he could have taken on the world single-handed and emerged victorious. Had picked up his father as if Pavlos weighed no more than an infant.

This one looked ill. Gaunt, hollow-eyed and barely able to support his own weight, let alone anyone else's. The sight paralyzed Emily. Left her speechless with dismay.

"Well, Emily?"

Collecting herself with a mighty effort, she said, "You haven't shaved in days."

The ghost of a smile touched his mouth. "Somehow, I'd expected a warmer welcome. Perhaps I should have stayed away longer."

"Perhaps you should have," she said, shock giving way to irrational anger. "Perhaps you shouldn't have come back at all."

His gaze drifted over her and came to rest on her face that she knew was ravaged with pent-up misery. "Emily, *karthula*," he murmured, a wealth of regret in his tone.

Her insides sagged. Melted into tears that flooded her eyes and washed her aching heart clean of everything but the burning need to touch him. To feel the tensile strength of muscle and bone beneath his clothing, the steady beat of the pulse at the corner of his jaw. To prove once and for all that she wasn't dreaming and he wasn't a ghost, he was real. "I didn't mean that," she cried, launching herself at him.

He grimaced and fended her off with an involuntary grunt of pain, reinforcing her initial impression that something was terribly wrong. His eyes, she noticed belatedly, held a feverish glint and a film of sweat beaded his upper lip.

"What happened to you?" she whispered.

His careless shrug turned into a flinch. "Just a minor scratch to my shoulder. Nothing to get excited about."

"I'll be the judge of that," she said, drawing him over the threshold.

He stepped inside, but staggered against a table just inside the door, sending it and the vase of flowers it held crashing to the marble floor. The noise brought Damaris and Giorgios running from the kitchen.

"I need a hand here," Emily panted, buckling under Niko's weight as she struggled to hold him upright. "Help me get him upstairs to a bed."

From the rear of the house, Pavlos spoke. "My room is closer. Bring him this way."

Between the three of them, they half-led, half-dragged Niko the length of the central hall and into the suite. As they eased him onto the bed, the front of his jacket fell open to reveal a spreading bloodstain on the upper left corner of his shirt.

The housekeeper gasped faintly but Emily immediately went into professional mode. "Pass me my scissors, Damaris," she ordered calmly, peeling off his jacket. "I'll have to cut away his shirt. Giorgios, I need clean towels, disinfectant and hot water."

Under the shirt she found a blood-soaked dressing covering a ragged puncture wound slightly to the right of his shoulder joint and just below his collarbone. "I'd say being shot amounts to a bit more than a minor scratch, Niko," she said, hoping nothing of her inner panic showed in her voice.

"What makes you think I've been shot?"

"I'm a nurse. I know a bullet injury when I see it, and this one's infected. A doctor needs to look at it."

"A doctor already has. Who do you think patched me up?"

"Someone in too much of a hurry from the looks of it. I'm taking you to the hospital."

He closed his eyes, weariness etched in every line of his face. "You'll do nothing of the sort. If I wanted to spend another night in a hospital, I wouldn't have had Dinos bring me here."

"I'm not Dinos, and I'm not taking any chances with your health."

"And I'm not a child."

"Then stop behaving like one and do as I ask."

"Forget it. I didn't just escape one hell to be thrown into another."

She looked for support from Pavlos who stood impassively at the foot of the bed, his gnarled old fingers gripping its rail. "For heaven's sake, will you talk some sense into your son, Pavlos?"

He shook his head. "No point trying, girl. His mind's made up."

Frustrated, she swung her attention back to Niko. "Fine. Have it your way. But don't blame me if you end up dead."

He opened his eyes a slit. "As if you'd let that happen, *karthula*. You're my angel of mercy."

"Let's see if you still think so after I'm finished with you."

She put on a pair of surgical gloves and began her task. As far as she could tell, he'd sustained no permanent damage. She found no sign of an exit point when she rolled him over on his side, which meant the bullet had lodged in his flesh and hopefully been removed by the doctor who'd treated him.

"Yeah," he mumbled, when she asked. "I told him he could hang it on his key chain."

He'd been lucky. As gunshot injuries went, she'd seen much worse, with major organs and bones damaged beyond repair. Nonetheless, the point where the bullet had entered his shoulder was ugly, with swelling around the sutures and angry red lines radiating from the wound site. And therein lay the reason for her alarm. "When did this happen, Niko?"

"A few days ago."

Typical vague answer, she thought, exasperated. "Were you hospitalized?"

"Overnight."

"Did you receive a tetanus shot?"

"*Neh*. In my other arm."

"Are you sure?"

"I was shot in the shoulder, Emily, not the brain. Yes, I'm sure. I can still feel where they shoved the needle in."

One piece of good news at least. "You'll be feeling this, as well," she warned, knowing she was going to hurt him. But he'd left her no choice. Bits of debris from the dressing and heaven only knew what else were adhered to his sutures and had to be removed. "It isn't going to be pleasant."

"Do what you have to do and get it over with," he ground out.

Brave words and nothing less than she'd expect from a man who refused to admit to any sort of weakness, but as she probed at the raw edges of his wound with surgical tweezers, then irrigated the area with warm water, the tendons on his neck stood out like cords.

Finally, with a clean dressing in place, she said, "That's about it for now."

"Good. Hand me my jacket and I'll be on my way."

He struggled to sit up, turned gray in the face and toppled back against the pillows.

Her patience snapped at that. "Try not to be a bigger fool than you already are, Niko Leonidas! The only place you're going is to bed, and you won't need your jacket for that."

He eyed her malevolently. "*Ade apo tho re,* Emily. You're beginning to annoy me."

"Not half as much as you're annoying me. Giorgios, grab his good arm and help me get him upstairs. We'll put him in the room adjoining mine—and I suggest," she added sweetly, addressing Niko again, "that you don't fight me on this. You've suffered enough pain for one night."

Although his glower was black as thunder, he offered no further resistance except to mutter, "Your bedside manner could use improvement, woman. Escaping rebel forces was a walk in the park compared to this."

But by the time they got him upstairs and into the bed Damaris had rushed to prepare, he had no fight left in him. "Clean sheets," he murmured on a ragged sigh. "Never thought they'd feel so good."

A moment later, he was asleep.

Emily left the connecting door between their rooms open and checked on him frequently during the remainder of the night, concerned as much about his rising temperature as the injury causing it. At one point, he opened his eyes and stared at her in the dim light as if he didn't know who she was. Another time, she heard him muttering her name deliriously and, placing the back of her hand against his cheek, realized he was burning up. Without knowing the extent of any vessel damage, she daren't give him aspirin and had to settle for sponging him down with tepid water. It helped temporarily, but never managed to subdue the fever completely.

From the outset, she'd known that what she could do for him would be, at best, a stopgap measure, and had hoped the new day would make him more amenable to accepting the kind of treatment only a physician could provide. But when, despite her efforts, his temperature spiked dangerously just before dawn, she knew she couldn't afford to wait for his permission, and phoned Pavlos's family physician.

She and the doctor had developed a strong mutual respect in the months since she'd come to Greece, and he brushed aside her apologies for disturbing him at such an ungodly hour. "I'll come at once," he said, after listening without interruption as she related the situation.

He arrived just as the sun was rising, subjected Niko

to a thorough examination, treated the infected gunshot wound and wrote out a prescription for topical and oral antibiotics. "Be glad you have a first-class nurse in residence, young man," he told Niko, when he was done. "You'd be hospitalized otherwise, whether or not you like it."

Then turning to Emily before he left, he added quietly, "Change his dressing regularly, and make sure he takes in plenty of fluids to replace what he's lost. If you're at all concerned that he's not getting enough, don't hesitate to call and we'll rehydrate him intravenously. Other than that, bed rest and medication should do the trick. Unless I hear from you sooner, I'll stop by again in the morning."

For two days, Emily was unconditionally happy. She had her man safe, close by and on the road to recovery. Although he slept a good part of the time, he always sensed when she was near. "Hey, angel," he'd murmur drowsily, fumbling for her hand, and her heart would swell with love.

The reprieve was short-lived. By the Thursday, he was chafing at being confined to bed and insisted that moving around was the best way to regain his strength. On Friday, he made it downstairs for breakfast, which was all it took for hostilities to resume between him and his father. And as usual, she found herself caught in the middle.

"What are you doing down here?" Pavlos demanded testily when he saw him.

"I have better things to do than lie around in bed all day, old man."

"Such as what?" Emily put in, horribly afraid she knew the answer.

"Unfinished business," he replied cryptically.

"If by that you mean going back to Africa and getting shot again, forget it."

"Don't tell me what to do, Emily. You're not my keeper."

"No, I'm the woman who loves you."

"More fool you," Pavlos chipped in, "because you have a jealous rival, my dear, and it's called death. He flirts with it constantly and has done for years."

"*Pre sto diavolo*—go to the devil, old man!" Niko retorted irascibly. "You know nothing about what motivates me, and even less about my relationship with Emily."

"I know she deserves a man willing to give her more than you ever will."

"Someone like you, I suppose?"

"At least she wouldn't be pacing the floor wondering where I am half the time."

"Because you can barely make it as far as the front door under your own steam."

They were like two lions fighting over the day's kill, the older one battling for dominance over a younger, more powerful adversary, and it sickened her.

"I could strangle the pair of you!" she exploded. "You're both so full of Greek pride, you can't see past it to what you're doing to one another. Or maybe you can, and you don't care."

"Stay out of it, Emily," Niko warned her. "This is between him and me."

"I won't!" she said, so angry she almost stamped her foot. "Pavlos is your father, for pity's sake, and you're his only child. You're all the family either of you has left and it's past time you put this senseless feud aside and made peace with one another. I know I would, were I in your place."

"But you're not," Niko said, so coldly that she shivered, "so can we agree to disagree and leave it at that? What you and I do in the bedroom is one thing, but you don't hear me interfering in your life the rest of the time. I'd appreciate it if you'd afford me the same sort of courtesy."

If he'd slapped her, she couldn't have been more shocked. "I thought we were about more than what happened in the bedroom."

He looked almost as shattered as she felt. "We are," he muttered, raking a furious hand through his hair. "I love you, you know that."

She'd once believed those three words were all it took for a man and a woman to make their relationship work, but she'd been wrong. They meant nothing if they came wrapped in resentment and soured what was once beautiful.

"Maybe you do," she said dully, "but not nearly enough."

CHAPTER ELEVEN

BEFORE he could respond to her accusation, let alone refute it, she was gone from the room. Seconds later, the front door slammed, drowning out the sound of her racing footsteps.

"That went well." Pavlos sneered. "Have anything planned for an encore?"

"Butt out," he growled, and turned to go after her.

"Do her a favor." The old man's voice followed him down the hall. "Let her alone. She's better off without you."

Maybe she was, but it wasn't in Niko's nature to give up without a fight. He'd be dead by now, if it were. And they'd invested too much of themselves in each other for it to end like this, over careless words spoken in the heat of the moment.

Wrenching open the door with his good hand, he stood on the step and shaded his eyes against the late morning sun. She'd already cleared the circular parking area and was swerving past an outraged peacock, which happened to be obstructing her path as she fled across the south lawn.

Intent on stopping her, Niko gave chase. Another dumb

move, he soon realized. Every bone in his body crunched as he hit the ground running. He covered no more than about forty meters before he was gasping for breath, and his shoulder was throbbing almost as badly as it had when he'd first been shot. He hadn't a hope of catching anything that moved, let alone a woman bent on putting as much distance between him and her as she was. And if that wasn't indignity enough, his father was now standing in the open doorway, watching the whole debacle.

"Emily!" The effort of raising his voice almost brought Niko to his knees.

She swung back to face him. *"What?"*

He couldn't answer. His lungs were bursting and black dots danced before his eyes. Humiliated by his weakness, not to mention his audience, he bent over, his chest heaving.

Seeing the shape he was in, she made her slow way back to him. "I already know how cruel you can be," she said, "but I had no idea you were stupid, too. You've probably made your wound bleed again and undone all the progress you made. Keep it up and you'll wind up in hospital, whether or not it's where you want to be."

"I want to be with you," he wheezed.

"Whatever for? We have nothing in common outside the bedroom, remember?"

"We both know that's not true."

"Then why did you say it?"

"Because I was—*am* frustrated as hell. I can no more tolerate not being in charge of my life than I can abide being on the receiving end of my father's grudging hospitality. The sooner I move back to the penthouse, the better for everyone."

"You're in no condition to go back to the penthouse," she informed him flatly.

"Too bad. I'm going anyway. Pavlos and I bring out the worst in each other. We always have." He grabbed at her hand. "Come with me, angel. It's Friday and we have the whole weekend ahead. Let's spend it together, making up for lost time."

"I don't know about that. Given your recent history, I doubt you're going to be feeling very…energetic."

"My upper torso might not be quite up to par, but below the waist everything's working just fine," he assured her. "Fully recovered or not, I want you so badly it hurts. More than that, I need you."

"You're only saying that to get your own way."

Annoyed, he snapped, "I thought you knew me better than that, Emily, but since you apparently don't, let me make one thing clear. I've yet to resort to lying in order to get a woman to sleep with me, and if you think that's what I'm doing now, then perhaps you should just keep running in the other direction and not look back." He released her hand and took a step away. "There, you're free. Off you go."

She bit her lip. A lone tear drizzled down her cheek. "I can't. I love you."

"Then why are we standing here arguing?"

"I don't know," she said and, closing the distance between them, buried her face against his neck.

"Go with him," Pavlos said, when she told him Niko was set on returning to the penthouse after lunch, then surprised her by adding, "and don't worry about being back here on Monday. Stay a week, or however long it takes to get him back on his feet. Judging from what I just saw, he's not quite the iron man he'd like to think he is."

"But you hired me to look after you," she protested, although they both knew he hadn't needed a resident nurse in days.

"Right now, he needs you a lot more than I do."

"I'm afraid you're right."

"Then pack a bag and be on your way. How are you getting into the city?"

"By taxi."

"No need. Giorgios will take you in the Mercedes. It'll be more comfortable for superhero."

She dropped a kiss on his cheek. "Thank you, Pavlos. You're an old softie under all that grump."

He swatted her away with rough affection. "Watch your mouth, girl, and don't be so quick with the gratitude. My son's about as cussed an individual as you could ask to meet, and I don't expect you'll have an easy time with him."

But she didn't care if she didn't have easy, as long as she had time.

They'd no sooner arrived at the penthouse than it started to pour with rain. Huge drops danced wildly on the terrace. Veils of cloud swirled outside the floor-to-ceiling windows, bringing an early dusk to the afternoon and obscuring the outside world. They didn't care. Wrapped in splendid isolation and with days of being together stretching before them, they didn't need sunshine. All they needed was each other.

That night, they sent out for dinner, ate it by candle-light and retired early. Knowing the day had wearied him, Emily didn't anticipate they'd make love, nor did she mind. She was happy simply to lie beside Niko in his big bed and feel the steady beat of his heart beneath her hand because, a week ago, she'd been afraid she'd never do so again. But he was alive, they were together, and that was all that mattered.

Proximity, though, was a powerful aphrodisiac and desire stole over them in quiet waves, with none of the tempestuous urgency they were used to. He turned on his side and his leg brushed hers, hair-roughened skin against smooth, warm thigh. His hand whispered over her hips to the hem of her short nightie and drew it up past her bottom. His mouth searched out hers and he uttered her name in muted invitation when she reached down and found him already hard.

All silken, pulsing heat, he positioned himself between her legs and slid inside her. They moved together in a slow, sweet symphony, adoring one another with soft murmurs of love. They climaxed in unison, the passion unspooling between them, lazy as waves rolling ashore. They fell asleep locked in each other's arms, sated with pleasure, and awoke to a morning washed clean and sparkling with sunshine.

So began a week she knew she would remember for the rest of her life. Sometimes they slept late. Other times, they went grocery shopping, arriving early at the markets to choose from a bewildering selection of food, and coming home loaded with goodies. Succulent lamb for souvlaki, or ground beef for moussaka. Fresh prawns and squid, cheese and olives for mezedes.

Ignoring Niko, who laughed and reminded her they were buying for two, not an army, she lingered at the fruit and vegetable stands, choosing jewel-toned egg-plant, vivid green peppers and bright red tomatoes, as well as lemons, tangerines and melons. She went to the bakery for bread still warm from the oven, and a quaint little shop at the entrance to the Plaka that sold honey, coffee, yogurt and nuts.

She learned to make tzaziki and saganaki. Even tried her hand at baklava. Although he had a housekeeper who usually came in every couple of days when he was in residence, Emily sent her away, preferring to change the bed linens and take care of the laundry herself, while Niko caught up by phone with what was happening at the airfield.

They took walks around the city. Visited museums and ancient churches. Explored art galleries and antique shops. Sometimes they'd go out for a meal. Mostly they stayed home, preferring to be alone.

They made love whenever and wherever the mood took them. Suddenly, urgently, in the late afternoon, on the rug in front of the fire in the living room, with the scent of burning apple wood filling the air. Sleepily, in the middle of the night, spurred by heaven only knew what dreams might have woken them. Wildly, hilariously, on the desk in his study, while he tried to conduct a serious phone conversation with Dinos at the office.

They lazed on the big overstuffed couch in the living room and read or listened to music, taking unhurried pleasure in simply being in the same room together.

It was like being married, except marriage was one subject they never discussed. To do so would have meant talking about the future which, in turn, would have brought that other world into focus. The one that took him away from her. Better to live in a fool's paradise.

But that dreaded other world intruded anyway, evidenced by a restlessness in him that increased as he regained his strength. Phone calls to the office weren't enough to satisfy him. He started spending time at the airfield again, an hour or two at first until, by the middle of the second week, he was back at work pretty much full-time. Domesticity had palled, even if his desire for her hadn't. He was raring for something more challenging than building fires or checking the firmness of tomatoes in the marketplace.

"I'm the boss," he said when she remonstrated with him. "Bosses are supposed to lead, not sit at home and let others do the job for them."

Matters came to a head on the third Sunday. All day, he'd been on edge. Finally, with evening closing in and Christmas carols playing on the stereo, he poured them each a glass of wine and came to sit next to her on the couch. "I have something to tell you, *karthula*," he began.

She knew what it was, without his having to elaborate. "You're leaving again."

"Yes."

"When?"

"Tomorrow."

"With so little advance notice?"

"Not exactly. I've known for a couple of days now that I'd be going."

"Where to this time?"

He looked at the fire, at the red roses she'd arranged in a vase on a side table, at the book lying facedown on the arm of the couch. He looked anywhere but at her, and her stomach turned over in a sickening lurch of prescience. "Oh, no," she whispered on a trembling breath. "Please tell me you're not going back to that horrendous place."

"I must," he said.

"Why? To get shot again, fatally this time?"

"People there are in terrible straits and they need help. And I need you to understand that I can't turn my back on them."

Anger welled up in her and she struck out at him, slamming her fist against his right arm. "What about what *I* need, Niko, or doesn't that matter to you?"

"I have given you all of myself."

"No. You give me what's left over after you take care of other people."

"Not so. You're what keeps me sane when the world around me erupts into madness. Before we met, I didn't care if I never came home. Now, I live for the time that we can be together again."

"Sure you do," she said, tears clogging her voice. "I'm the warm body that makes you forget the horrors you left behind, but it doesn't change the fact that you care more about strangers than you'll ever care about me."

"I don't deserve that, Emily."

"I don't deserve to be left waiting and wondering if you'll come back to me in one piece or a body bag."

"No, you don't," he said, setting down his wine and going to stand at the glass doors leading to the terrace, "which is why I never promised you forever. I've always known I couldn't give it to you."

So there it was, the end of the affair, delivered with the

uncompromising honesty that was his trademark. They'd finally run out of borrowed time and the tomorrow she'd tried so hard to postpone stood on the doorstep.

Hollow with pain, she said, "We were never a good fit, were we?"

"Never," he admitted, after a horrible, tension-filled pause.

"Always a ships-passing-in-the-night sort of thing."

"That about covers it."

But his voice was all rusty, as if he'd choked on a peanut. And she…she was perilously close to sobbing. She had followed in her parents' footsteps and gambled everything for the pleasure of living in the moment. And in doing so had lost everything. Their biggest mistake had become hers, too.

"So…o…o." She drew out the word on a long, quivering sigh. "I guess this is goodbye."

"I guess it is."

"It's for the best."

"Probably."

She dug her fingernails into her palms; bit the inside of her lip until she tasted blood. "I'll collect my stuff and get out of here. You must have a lot to do and don't need me underfoot."

He didn't argue, just straightened his shoulders and turned back to confront her, his face unreadable. "Fine. I'll drive you back to the villa."

And subject them both to more suffering? "No," she said. "There's a taxi stand right outside your building. I'll take a cab."

She left her untouched wineglass next to his and went upstairs to the bedroom to throw clothes, shoes and toiletries haphazardly into her suitcases. She had to get away quickly, before she fell down on her knees and begged him not to leave her.

At last she was ready. All that remained to be done was walking away from him. If there'd been a back entrance to the penthouse, she'd have taken it and spared them both the agony of a last goodbye, but he remained in the living room which opened off the long hall leading to the foyer.

"I think I've got everything," she said, staring straight ahead because, if she looked into his jade-green eyes one more time, she'd lose it completely.

"Anything you've forgotten, I'll send to the villa."

"Thanks." She swallowed painfully. "Take care of yourself."

"You, too."

She tried to open the door. Fumbled with a latch, which refused to budge. Was dimly aware of movement in the room behind her and renewed her efforts, not wanting him to come and help.

She could not look at him, or speak to him, or let him come near her again. She could not.

Eyes streaming, she made one last effort. The blasted latch clicked, but still the door refused to budge because, she realized, staring blurrily through her tears, he was holding it shut. Over the tormented thud of her heart she heard his voice so close behind her that his breath wafted warm and damp over her nape. "Emily, don't go," he begged. "It doesn't have to end like this."

She wilted, empty of pride and so full of hurt that she had no fight left in her. Dropping her luggage, she turned in his arms and clung to him, accepting that she was as helpless to refuse him as she was to change the course he'd set himself long before he met her. "I'm so afraid for you," she sobbed.

"I know, sweetheart," he said, kissing her eyes, her tears. "I know."

Hounded by the remorseless hunger, which had held them in thrall from the first, they sought the only comfort left to them and went at each other like mad things, giving the lie to any notion that being apart was better than being together. She clawed at him, desperate in her need, raking her hands down his shirt-front to tear open the buttons. He pinned her against the door, yanked up her skirt and ripped off her panties. Freeing himself from his jeans, he hoisted her off her feet, pulled her legs around his waist, and drove into her as if she was all that stood between him and damnation.

After that, there was no question of her leaving. Instead they tried to do what they'd done so successfully for over two weeks. They tried to play house.

He sorted the clothes he'd take with him in the morning. She folded them, the way a good wife would, and put them neatly in the canvas carryall that held enough to see him through as many days as he'd be gone. Too many, she noticed, counting three pairs of jeans, eight shirts and as many changes of undershorts and socks.

They tried to talk about anything except where he'd be tomorrow night at that time, but the conversation stalled at every turn and they'd subside into stricken silence before making another valiant attempt at normality.

They sat down to dinner, but abandoned the table when neither of them could eat. Their gazes met and held, and broke apart again when the emotion in their depths threatened to overwhelm them.

"Let's stop this," he finally said. "Come to bed, *khriso mou*. Let me hold you in my arms and love you one last time before I go."

She tried, fusing her body with his in a desperate, hopeless attempt to stop time. Amassing his every word, his every touch, and hoarding them against an empty future. She wished she could shut down her mind and simply listen to her body. But the specter of his flying off into the teeth of danger, of death, haunted her. It left her drained, deprived of everything that gave her life meaning. "Please don't go," she finally beseeched him. "If you love me at all, please stay and keep me with you."

"I can't," he said.

And she couldn't, either. He was an adventurer, at heart as much a rebel as those he fought against, albeit for different reasons. Risking life and limb gave him a rush she'd never understand. She needed stability—a real home, a husband, children—and she couldn't live suspended indefinitely on the fine edge of sanity, wanting what he couldn't give her.

Light from the en suite bathroom filtered into the room, crowding the corners with shadows but providing enough illumination for her to watch him sleeping. With the hours racing by much too fast, she committed to memory the curve of his mouth, the clean line of his jaw and cheekbones, his lashes, so long and thick he could sweep a street with them.

Beyond the windows, the sky grew imperceptibly lighter, precursor of a new and hellish dawn shouting that today was their last day. She did not want to hear or see it, and closing her eyes, she pressed her body close to his, inhaling through every pore the very essence of all that he was.

6:30 a.m.

Time to make a move.

Deactivating the alarm clock before it disturbed the silence, Niko took a moment to savor the warmth of her body next to his. Feigning sleep himself, he'd listened to her crying softly throughout the night. It had taken every last milligram of self-control for him not to reach for her and tell her what he knew she wanted to hear.

I'll send someone else in my place, and stay with you. We'll get married, make a home together, raise a family.

Exhaustion had claimed her before temptation got the better of him. Now she slept, with strands of her pale blond hair spread over his shoulder as if to bind him to her. She looked young, beautiful. Defenseless as a child, and unutterably sad.

He had done that to her. What had started out to be no more than a harmless flirtation designed to show Pavlos that his trust in her was misplaced, had blossomed out of control. Niko had seen it coming, but had done nothing to put an end to it. She had captivated him like no other woman he'd ever met, and he'd made the fatal mistake of falling in love with her.

Worse, selfish bastard that he was, he'd let her fall in love with him. And now he had to leave her because he knew that happy-ever-after wasn't in the cards. Of his fifteen employees, ten were pilots. The youngest was single and still living at home. Five of the remaining nine were divorced, victims of a career that demanded too much of the women who'd once loved them enough to take their names and bear their children.

He did not want that for her, for them. He'd rather lose her now, with the good memories still intact, than wait until all the joy and passion had turned bitter with resentment.

6:31 a.m.

Stealthily he eased himself off the bed, collected his clothes and, as he'd done before, went downstairs to shower and dress in the guest suite. As a rule, he stood under the jets an indecently long time because there was no telling when he'd next have access to hot water or clean towels. But that morning he made quick work of preparing for the day ahead.

6:49 a.m.

Ready to go. A better man than he'd ever be would have picked up his bag and left. He couldn't go without a last farewell, and went to the library to find pen and paper.

I love you enough to set you free to live the kind of life you're looking for, he wrote. *The man who can give it to you will be lucky indeed. Be happy, Emily.*

Then stopping by the living room, he plucked a rose from the bouquet she'd arranged, and stole back upstairs.

She lay exactly as he'd left her. He ached to kiss her. To whisper her name. To taste her mouth one more time.

For once, he did the right thing. He placed the note and the rose on his pillow and left her.

CHAPTER TWELVE

"HE'S gone again," Pavlos said, his wise old eyes absorbing everything in a single glance. "He's left you."

Too awash in misery to put a brave face on things, Emily collapsed into the chair next to his. "Yes."

"So what now?"

"I think I must go, too, Pavlos. There's nothing more for me here." Except a rose already wilting, a note that put a final end to hope and a heart in shreds.

"There's me."

She shook her head sadly. "I've taken advantage of your generosity too long already."

"Rubbish! You nursed me back to health, put up with my bad temper and—"

"And now you're well again." Or as well as he'd ever be. His hip had healed to a degree, but his eighty-six-year-old body was worn-out, and there wasn't a thing she or anyone else could do about it.

"You gave me a reason to get out of the bed in the morning," he insisted. "I've grown fond of you. You're like a daughter to me and will always have a place in my home."

For a moment, she was tempted. To be needed,

wanted; to be part of a family, however small…hadn't she longed for just such peace of mind and heart ever since she was nine? But common sense told her she'd find neither in this house. She'd never hear the doorbell without hoping it was Niko come to tell her he'd changed his mind, that he wanted forever after all, and he wanted it with her.

If Pavlos had been truly alone, it might have been different, but he had the devoted Giorgios and Damaris to take care of his daily needs, and a family doctor who visited three times a week. She'd be leaving him in good hands.

"I'm fond of you, too, and I'll never forget your kindness," she told him gently, "but my life is in Vancouver. I have a house there. Friends, a career, financial and professional obligations to honor."

"And I'm not enough to make you turn your back on them." He sighed and nodded acceptance. "Will you keep in touch?"

"Of course."

"I don't suppose I have to tell you that my son is a fool."

"No more than I was, Pavlos."

"I tried to warn you, girl."

"I know you did."

The trouble was, his warning had come too late. It had been too late from the moment she and Niko had set eyes on each other. The attraction between them had blazed out of control, instantaneous combustion bent on destroying anything that stood in its path. The fear that she might live to regret giving in to it had dissolved in the lilting excitement, the sheer *aliveness* of being in love. Nothing compared to it.

What she hadn't known was that when it ended, it

took more than it had ever bestowed. Without Niko she was empty, incomplete. She had known him less than three months and in that time he had turned her life upside down, stolen everything she had to give, and left her with nothing.

Or so she believed when she said goodbye to Pavlos. And perhaps, if she'd chosen a different career, she might have ascribed the mood swings and exhaustion she brought home with her to the unavoidable emotional fall-out of a love affair gone wrong. But nursing school had taught her well. She was attuned to her body and as the old year came to an end, she hardly needed a home pregnancy test to confirm the cause of the fatigue and faint but undeniable nausea that hounded her every waking hour.

The future Niko had insisted no one could predict was staring her in the face with a certainty that eliminated any possibility that she might one day come to forget him. He would be with her always in the shape of his child.

The realization shattered the blessed numbness, which had cushioned her since the day he'd left. She was a twenty-seven-year-old, highly trained medical professional, for pity's sake! Of all people, she should have known how to protect herself from an unplanned pregnancy. How could she have been so careless?

Except she hadn't been, nor had Niko. Even at their most spontaneous they'd taken precautions, to the point that he'd joked about buying condoms in bulk, to cut down on the number of trips to the drugstore! But there'd been a few times during their last two weeks together that they'd almost left it too late to be safe. Idiot that she was to have exposed herself to such risks, she must have conceived then.

Her doctor, whom she went to see in late January, soon put paid to that theory. "You're well into your second trimester, Emily. About sixteen weeks along, I'd say."

"I can't be." Unless…had they cut things too fine on the boat? Been too carried away by the newness of their affair to be as responsible as they should have been?

"Are you sure you last menstruated at the end of October?"

"Pretty sure," she said, vaguely recalling her period had been lighter than usual. Nothing more than spotting, but she hadn't paid much attention at the time. She'd been too busy falling in love.

"What about the father?"

"What about him?"

"Are you going to tell him?"

"No."

"Why not?"

"Because we're not together anymore. He's not into parenthood, at least with me."

That night, she lay in bed, surrounded by all the comforting things that spelled home. The blue and white toile de jouy wallpaper she'd hung herself. The handmade wedding ring quilt she'd bought at auction, three years ago. Her reproduction four-poster bed and matching rosewood bombe chest of drawers. The silver-framed photograph of her parents and two small oil paintings she'd found at an estate sale, the summer she'd graduated from nursing school.

They were proof she didn't need a man around, she

told herself. Closer to her due date she'd put a rocking chair in the alcove near the window, where she'd nurse her baby, and a white bassinet next to her bed. When he grew too big for that, she'd turn the second bedroom into a nursery. Paint clouds on the ceiling. Stencil unicorns and pixies on the walls—oh, and a guardian angel, because every child had to have a guardian angel, even if he couldn't have a father.

A father...Niko...

Memories of him rushed to the forefront of her mind. Of his warm breath tickling her neck when he leaned over to kiss her good morning. His mouth against hers, his voice in her ear.

Of his long, strong body and olive skin. The planes of his chest, the swell of muscle over his shoulder, the lean, taut curve of his buttocks.

Of his beautiful face, and his mesmerizing eyes and the way they turned dark when the passion he tried so hard to contain rode roughshod over him.

Of his laughter, his wicked sense of humor... *You've left me with an erection that would do a stallion proud, Emily....*

Oh, to hear him laugh again! To see him, to hold him!

As winter turned to spring, she struggled to put the past behind her, but it wasn't easy with his baby growing inside her. Wouldn't have been even if she wasn't pregnant.

Any mention of humanitarian aid brought him vividly alive in her mind. A melody they'd listened to together, the scent of aftershave on another man, a stranger, when it belonged only to him, were enough to turn a good day bad. He was in her heart, in her soul.

But in every other respect, she was alone. Alone and

pregnant, because although he'd paid lip service to loving her, when put to the test, the father of her unborn child chose to risk life and limb in some benighted corner of the world, rather than risk his heart to her.

Well, let him, she'd tell herself, furious at her own weakness. She'd had her fill of reluctant charity, growing up as she had in her aunt's house where she'd never been welcome. If Niko couldn't commit to her without reservation, she didn't want him at all.

Anger was so much easier to bear than grief, even if they did both boil down to the same thing in the end.

"Will you be able to manage financially?" her friends asked when they heard she was about to become a single parent.

"Yes," she said, the irony not escaping her that her baby's grandfather was responsible for the substantial savings she'd amassed. "I have it all planned out. I can work for another five months, then after the birth, take a year's maternity leave, and when that ends, hire a live-in nanny to look after the baby."

But her calculations misfired. On the twelfth of May when she was only thirty-three weeks into her pregnancy, and contrary to anything she or her doctors had reason to expect, she gave birth to a three pound, eleven ounce daughter.

As a nurse, she knew that a mildly preterm baby's chances of surviving without lasting complications were excellent. As a mother, she wore herself to a shadow fretting over the tiny, delicate creature who had taken her heart by storm from the second she entered the world.

She named her Helen and brought her home when

she weighed five pounds. "At least she looks all there," the well-meaning woman next door remarked, stopping by the next day to inspect the new arrival. "For a preemie, that is."

Emily's friends were somewhat more encouraging. "She's adorable, so petite and feminine," they agreed, flocking around the bassinet.

To Emily, she was the most beautiful baby ever born. She brought light to a life which, since the day Niko left, had been too often filled with darkness. Sitting in the rocking chair, with her baby at her breast and the dogwood trees blooming outside the window, Emily found a measure of peace that had eluded her for much too long.

Spring melded into summer. If it wasn't too hot, Emily would tuck Helen into her stroller and take her for walks in the park or along the seawall. She'd nurse her in the shade of a sun umbrella on the patio.

She'd kept her promise to stay in touch with Pavlos, and at first they'd exchanged frequent e-mails but, as the months came and went, they'd written to each other less often. He never mentioned Niko, had little to say about anything really, and she decided against telling him about her pregnancy. What was the point in upsetting him?

After Helen was born, she wasn't so sure she'd made the right decision. Would learning he was a grandfather bring a little joy into Pavlos's life, or merely create an even deeper rift between father and son? More to the point, could he keep it a secret from Niko?

She had no doubt that, should he find out she'd had his baby, Niko would feel obligated to do the honorable thing and marry her. And that, she knew, would merely invite long-term misery for everyone. He would never

settle happily for domesticity, and she wouldn't—
couldn't live with his career choice. No child needed a
daredevil for a father. Better to have no father at all than
one who, as Pavlos had once pointed out, flirted with
death every time he went to work.

As summer advanced, Helen continued to thrive.
Although still small for her age, she gained weight
steadily, clocking in at over six and a half pounds when
she was three months old.

One morning, Emily had put her down for her
morning nap and was folding laundry at the kitchen
counter when she received a distraught phone call from
Giorgios. Pavlos had taken a turn for the worse and was
not expected to recover. He had refused to be admitted
to hospital and was asking for her.

"What about his son?" she said. "Has he been con-
tacted?"

"We have tried, but he is far away."

Typical! she thought. Why stick close to home and
your ailing father, when you could be somewhere else
giving your all to strangers?

"Will you come, Emily?"

How could she refuse? Pavlos needed her. "Yes, but
it'll take me a little time to make the arrangements."

"I am afraid he does not have much time left."
Giorgios's voice broke. "He is tired of fighting to live,
Emily. Many times, he asks me, 'What for do I wake up
each morning to an empty house?'"

"You tell him he has to hold on," she said fiercely.
"Don't you dare let him die before I get there."

* * *

She and Helen arrived at the villa by taxi two days later. Obtaining a passport for her baby at such short notice had taken some doing, but Emily had appealed to a sympathetic government official who, when he'd heard her situation, had cut through the bureaucratic red tape in record time.

As the cab rounded the last curve in the driveway and the villa came into view, nothing seemed to have changed. The palm trees rose tall against the deep blue sky. The flower beds blazed with color under the sun. Proud as ever, the peacocks strutted over the immaculate lawns.

Inside, the house told a different story. The atmosphere was somber, oppressive, although her showing up with a baby caused something of a stir.

"Yes, she's mine," Emily said to a stunned Damaris. Then, to Giorgios, "Am I in time?"

"*Neh*. When he heard you were coming, he found new strength. He is awake and just a few minutes ago asked how soon you would be here."

Lifting Helen from her infant seat, she said, "Then let's not keep him waiting any longer."

She had witnessed death in all its guises many times in her career, but even though she thought herself prepared, she was shocked when she saw Pavlos. He lay against his pillows, so frail and shrunken that a stiff breeze could have blown him away. His face was the color of parchment, his eyes closed, and had it not been for the shallow rise and fall of his chest, he might have already been dead.

"Hold her for me for a second, will you?" she whispered, passing Helen to Damaris, and approached his bed. "Hello, darling," she said softly.

He opened his eyes. "You came," he said, his voice a pale imitation of what it once had been.

"Of course."

"You're a good girl."

Stifling a rush of grief, she took Helen from Damaris and laid her in his arms. "I've brought someone with me," she said. "Say hello to your grand-daughter, Pavlos."

He gazed at Helen who stared up at him from big blue eyes. Almost inaudibly, he whispered, "She is Niko's child?"

"Yes."

Tears trickled down his face. "I never thought to see the day. *Yiasu, kali egoni.* Hello, my little one."

"Her name's Helen."

"A good Greek name." The breath rattled in his belea-guered lungs. "A beautiful name for a beautiful child."

"I thought you'd approve."

He tore his eyes away from Helen. "How could I not? She is of my blood and has you for her mother. Tell me all about her."

"Tomorrow," she said, seeing that he was tiring fast. "For now, Pavlos, try to get some sleep."

He groped for her hand. "Sleep will come soon enough, girl, and we both know it is not one from which I will awake. Talk to me while there is still time. I want to know everything."

"Stay with him," Damaris murmured, scooping Helen into her arms again. "I will look after the little one."

"Take Giorgios with you when you go," Pavlos

wheezed. "His mournful face and death bed vigil weary me."

"Poor man," Emily said, when they were alone. "He loves you so much, Pavlos, and all this…" She indicated the oxygen tank and other hospital paraphernalia in the room. "It probably scares him."

"I know, and it hurts me that he is so overwrought. I would spare him seeing me like this, if I could. He has been more of a son to me than Niko ever was."

"Niko loves you, too."

"Save me the platitudes, girl! I am dying. If he cares about me at all, why is he the only one not here now?"

Footsteps crossing the adjoining sitting room came to a halt in the open doorway. "But I *am* here," Niko said. "I came as soon as I heard."

CHAPTER THIRTEEN

HORRIFIED, Emily froze, battered by panic and such a welter of conflicting emotions that her instinct was to run as far and as fast as she could to escape him. Anything to suppress the surge of longing aroused by the sound of his voice, the craving to touch him again. Anything to prevent his finding out about Helen. But what if he'd already seen her and recognized her as his? And even if he hadn't, how could she justify leaving Pavlos when he was clutching her hand so desperately?

Reining in her emotions, she drew on the control which had served her so well as a critical care nurse. With deceptive calm, she swiveled in the chair and in one sweeping glace took in everything about him from the top of his head to his dusty flight boots.

He looked like hell. Fatigue smudged his eyes, he hadn't shaved in days and he needed a haircut. Judging by their appearance, he must have slept in his jeans and shirt longer than was good for them or him, and the crystal was cracked on his flight computer watch. But more than all else, he looked unutterably sad.

"I'll leave the pair of you alone together," she muttered, rising to her feet.

"No," Pavlos wheezed, his eyes beseeching her.

Niko crossed the room and pressed her down on the chair again. "Please stay, angel," he said. "What I have to say is as much for you as for my father."

"Don't you dare upset him."

"I won't."

He pulled a chair close on the far side of the bed and took his father's other hand. The contrast between them, the one so big and strong and deeply tanned, the other so weak, with every vein showing through the paper-thin skin, was painfully moving to behold.

"If you're here to dance on my grave," Pavlos said, the faintest spark of the old hostility charging his words, "you needn't have rushed. I'm not dead yet."

"And I thank God for that, *Patera*, because I want to tell you I'm sorry I've made such a poor job of being your son."

"An *epiphaneia* at this late date?" Pavlos let out a croak of feeble laughter. "What brought that on?"

"I have just come back from a hell where political corruption and genocide rule the day. I've witnessed mothers ripped away from their newborn infants, fathers murdered before their children's eyes and been powerless to prevent either. I've met thousands of orphans infected by diseases, which will kill them before they grow to be adults. I have buried a dead baby and wept over his grave because there was no one else to mourn him."

Momentarily overcome, he cleared his throat and rubbed his thumb lightly over the back of his father's hand. "In the end, the devastation and ruin defeated me. What was I doing, trying to mend broken families in a foreign country when my own was falling apart at home? By what right had I held you at a distance, *Patera*, when your greatest sin was wanting to give me a better life than you had when you were young?"

"You're my son," Pavlos said. "Stubborn and proud and hell set on making your own way in the world, just as I was at your age. And you wanted to make that world a better place."

"Yes, I did. But I neglected you in the process. Have I left it too late to ask your forgiveness?"

With great effort, Pavlos lifted his other hand and laid it alongside Niko's stubble-covered jaw. "Ah, my foolish boy," he said hoarsely. "Don't you know it's never too late for a father to welcome his son home again?"

Niko started to cry then, harsh, horrible, rasping sobs that tore through his body. Emily couldn't bear it. Springing up from her chair, she stumbled to the French doors in the sitting room and ran out to the terrace.

At the far end, a path led away from the villa and wound through the gardens to a marble bench set in a shady arbor screened from the house by a grove of lemon trees. Reaching it, she sank down on the seat's cool, hard surface and wrestled with the demons plaguing her.

She had fought so hard to get over Niko. To shut herself off from dreams of him vivid enough that she awoke with the scent of his skin, the silken touch of his intimate flesh, taunting her. She'd struggled to find a foothold in a world without him. To build a safe, secure, contented life around her baby.

And for what? To fall for him all over again in less time than it took to blink, swayed by tears she'd never thought to see him shed, and words she'd never believed she'd hear him utter? Casting aside his indomitable pride, he'd revealed his innermost heart and in so doing, had walked right back into hers.

She could not allow it. Could not risk being dragged back into the morass of misery where loving him had landed her before. She had a child to protect now. Helen needed a mother who was whole, not half a woman pining for what she couldn't have. If she acted quickly and discreetly, she could leave the villa without anyone being the wiser. It was the best thing, the only thing to do.

Mind made up, she went around the side of the house to let herself in the front door, and came face-to-face with a harassed Georgios. "I've been looking for you, Emily. Your little one is screaming with hunger and Damaris cannot comfort her."

Right on cue, Emily's breasts started to leak and a quick glance at the clock on the wall showed her it had been over two hours since she'd last nursed her baby. Leaving would have to be postponed a little longer. "Please ask Damaris to bring her to me in the drawing room. It's cooler in there."

"If you'd rather be upstairs, everything's ready in your suite."

"Thanks, Giorgios," she said, "but now that Niko's arrived, I won't be staying here after all."

"Pavlos will be disappointed."

"I don't think so. We had our time together. Now it's his son's turn."

Niko sat with his father until he drifted off to sleep, then quietly left the bedroom and went in search of Emily. He and Pavlos had made peace at last. Now it was time to mend things with her. He'd hurt her badly. Hurt them both, for reasons which, in retrospect, struck him as unforgivably egotistical on his part. Well, no more. Things would be different from now on.

The house was silent as a tomb. An unfortunate comparison, he thought with a pang. Already the scent of death, indefinable but all too familiar, pervaded the atmosphere. But as he drew level with the pillared entrance to the formal day salon, a place so seldom used that he couldn't remember the last time he'd set foot in it, a soft, dovelike murmur caught his attention.

Thinking a bird might have flown in from the garden, he stepped quietly into the room and instead discovered Emily sitting by the open window, a lightweight shawl of some sort draped over her shoulder, her head bent attentively over the infant at her partially exposed breast.

The shock almost felled him. Yes, he'd urged her to find a man who could give her what he'd thought he never could, but not once in all the months they'd been apart had it occurred to him that she'd take his advice to heart so quickly or so thoroughly.

As though sensing she was being observed, she looked up and caught him staring. Her eyes widened and quickly, almost defiantly, she drew the shawl over the baby—a newborn, from what he'd been able to observe, probably no more than a few weeks old.

"Well," he said, affecting amusement when what he most wanted to do was howl with disappointed outrage, "I hardly expected this."

She tilted one shoulder in a dismissive little shrug. "What can I say? The day's been full of surprises."

He angled a glance at the baby, although all he could

see were its tiny legs and the little red soles of its feet poking out beneath the shawl. "Boy or girl?"

"Girl."

"Does she look like you?"

"Some people think so."

"Lucky her. And you're happy?"

"Deliriously. I have everything I ever wanted."

"Really?" He'd never have guessed. She was fidgety, tense, the picture of uneasiness. Rearranging the shawl needlessly. Looking anywhere but at him.

There was something else not right about the picture of contentment she was trying to present, and watching the nervous fluttering of her fingers, he all at once realized what it was. "In that case," he said, "why aren't you wearing a wedding ring?"

Of all the questions she'd feared he might ask, this one had never crossed her mind, and she briefly considered trying to come up with an inspired lie to throw him off the scent. Since she'd done such a good job of fooling him into thinking she'd found some other man to take his place, why not continue with the charade? But suddenly she'd had enough of the deceit and the subterfuge. She'd tell him the truth, or at least an edited version of it, and if he persisted in leaping to all the wrong conclusions, that was hardly her problem. "Because I'm not married," she said.

"Why not?"

"I rushed into a relationship with the wrong man, we went our separate ways and I'm bringing up my baby alone. Don't look so disapproving. It was my choice, and hardly unique in today's world. Hundreds of women make the same decision every day."

"You're not one of those women, Emily," he said. "You should have held out for the husband you always wanted."

"Well, I didn't. I had a baby instead."

His unforgettable green eyes scoured her face, undermining her resolve to remain coolly disinterested. "It's not too late for you to have both."

"I'm afraid it is. There aren't too many men out there willing to take on another man's child."

"There's me," he said. "If you'll have me, I'll marry you."

She was so unprepared for his answer that she almost dropped Helen. "Don't be ridiculous! The Niko Leonidas I know doesn't invest in marriage."

"That man doesn't exist anymore. He grew up and learned what was important in life."

"He used to believe helping those in need was important."

"He still does."

Bristling, she said, "I'm not in need, Niko. I can manage very well on my own."

"You misunderstand. What I'm saying is that I haven't abandoned the causes I've supported all these years. I still believe in doing my part and I always will. I just don't need to keep proving it by playing Russian roulette with my own life. There are other, more effective ways to make a difference."

"Marrying me isn't one of them," she said. But oh, how she wished it were!

He crossed the room in swift strides and came to where she sat. "Listen to me," he implored. "I love you. Give me a chance to show you how much. Let me make a home for you and your baby. Let me be a father to her. I don't care who else's blood runs in her veins. That she's yours is reason enough for me to love her as if she were my own."

"Oh...!" She pressed her trembling lips together and fought to hold back the tears. "This is so not what I expected when I woke up this morning."

"Me, neither. If you need time to think about it—"

"We both do, Niko. Right now your father needs you more than I do, and you're too emotionally fragile to be making any other major decisions."

"Not to the point that I don't know my own mind. In deference to my father, I won't pressure you to accept my proposal now, but I won't be put off indefinitely."

"There's more at issue here than just you and me, Niko. My situation...well, it's not exactly what you think."

"Do you love me?"

"Yes."

"Are you married?"

"I've already told that I'm not."

"Then there are no issues that can't be worked out."

He ran his hands down his crumpled shirt and dusty jeans. "Look, I'm a mess, inside and out. I'm going home to get cleaned up and pull myself together, but in the event that you're worried my proposal is some spur-of-the-moment impulse on my part—"

"Is it? You are a man who likes to rush to the rescue, after all."

"The person I'm rescuing this time is myself, Emily. It's taken me a long time, but I've finally set my priorities straight. Only a fool discards the treasures that bless his life. I was on my way home to tell my father that even before I heard he was dying. To my lasting regret, I've left it too late to make it up to him for all the wasted years. I won't make the same mistake with you."

He left her then, but not as he had before. Not empty of everything but despair. She'd once read that when it rains in the desert, all the cacti burst into glorious flower. For such a long time her spirit had been arid as a desert, but his words made hope bloom in every corner of her heart and fill it to overflowing.

While he was gone, Giorgios came to tell her Pavlos was awake again. She went to him immediately.

His tired eyes brightened when he saw she'd brought Helen with her and he tried to reach out to hold her, but the effort was too much for him and he sank back against the pillows. His pulse was weak and erratic, his breathing labored as his poor old heart struggled to keep working, and he soon drifted asleep again.

Niko joined her not long after and took up his post on the other side of the bed.

Sensing his presence, Pavlos muttered haltingly, "You here, son?"

"I'm here, *Babas*."

"You'll be a rich man when I go."

"Not as rich as I'd be if you stayed."

"Not enough time left for that, boy. It's up to you and Emily now."

"I know."

"You take good care of her."

"I will."

"And my granddaughter. Be a better father to her than I ever was to you."

Startled, Niko shot Emily a quick glance, but he said only, "I won't let you down, *Babas*."

"Never have, boy," Pavlos said, his voice barely above a whisper. "Always made me proud...should have told you before now."

He never spoke. He subsided into sleep again, deeper this time, his respirations so shallow they barely moved the sheet covering him. Emily busied herself checking the IV solution and oxygen, hoping to avoid the inevitable question about his father's comment, but Niko's attention remained fixed on Pavlos.

An hour passed, and then another. Helen squirmed and scrunched up her face, the prelude, Emily knew, to a very vocal demand for food. "I'll nurse her in the other room so she doesn't disturb him," she told Niko.

"Don't take too long," he said.

Afternoon slipped toward dusk. Giorgios brought tea and sandwiches. Damaris took Helen and put her to bed in a drawer she'd taken from a dresser, which was lined with soft blankets. The doctor paid a call, met Emily's gaze, shook his head regretfully and said he'd be by again in the morning.

Throughout the night, Emily and Niko kept vigil. Lost in their own thoughts of the man who'd made such an indelible impression on them both, they spoke little. At six o'clock the next morning, Pavlos died.

"He's gone, Niko," she said. "It's over."

He nodded, bent his head and gathered his father's frail body in his arms.

Leaving him to make his private farewell, she slipped from the room and went out to the terrace. In the half-light of dawn, the flower beds shone like pale clumps of stars. It was going to be another beautiful late August day. The first of many without Pavlos.

She didn't hear Niko join her until he spoke. "He was rambling, wasn't he, when he said the baby's mine?"

"No," she said, too sad and exhausted to prevaricate. The truth had to come out sooner or later, it might as well be now. "You're her biological father."

"That's impossible. We always used protection."

"We couldn't have been as careful as we thought,"she said.

"How old is she? She looks practically newborn."

"She's three months old."

"How much does she weigh?"

"Nearly seven pounds now, but she was less than four at birth. She looks small because she was born seven weeks early."

He almost staggered. "Why didn't you tell me?"

"I tried to when you found me with her yesterday. You wouldn't let me."

"I'm not talking about yesterday afternoon, Emily. I'm talking about the last nine or ten months. I would have married you at once, if I'd known."

"I know you would. I didn't want you on those terms. I still don't."

"I was afraid that might be the reason," he said. "I seem to have a real talent for screwing up the relationship that means the most to me."

And he walked back into the house, a man so bowed down with sorrow that she couldn't bear to watch him.

CHAPTER FOURTEEN

SHE saw little of him in the week that followed. Arranging the funeral and the myriad tasks associated with it kept him occupied. Pavlos had many business associates and the stream of callers coming to the villa to pay their respects was endless.

Emily helped poor Damaris, who was run off her feet providing refreshments, and spent many quiet hours in the gardens with Helen, wondering what the future held. Although he'd made time to get to know his daughter, Niko treated Emily more like a sister than a lover. Had she ruined their chances by keeping their baby a secret? she wondered.

She received her answer when he sought her out as she sat in the shade of an olive tree, on the lawn overlooking the Saronic Gulf. For the last two days, they'd had the villa to themselves again, but it was too lovely an afternoon to spend indoors.

"We've pretty much laid the past to rest, Emily," he announced, dropping down beside her on the blanket she'd spread on the grass. "Now we have to take care of the future. I said I wouldn't rush you for an answer to my proposal, and I've tried to keep my distance, but I'm afraid I've run out of patience."

Her mouth dropped open. "Are you saying you still want to marry me?"

"More than I've ever wanted anything in my life. The question is, do you trust me enough to want to marry me?"

"Why wouldn't I trust you?"

"Well, let's see. I showed myself to be devious and un-scrupulous by trying to expose you as a fraud. I seduced you, then agreed that we weren't a good match and might as well end our relationship. I left you, and you had a baby you didn't dare tell me about because you quite rightly thought I'd make a lousy father. Shall I go on?"

"No. We've laid the past to rest, remember, so let's do as you suggest and talk about the future."

"Okay. Here's what I've decided. Although I'll continue to support the causes I hold dear, I'm retiring as a pilot and sharing management of the company with Dinos. I intend to take an active role in overseeing my father's investments as he always wished me to do. Giorgios and Damaris have been very loyal to my family, so if you and I get married and you're agreeable, I'd like to live here and keep them and the rest of staff on. How am I doing so far?"

"Very well. I couldn't ask for better."

"Is that a yes to my proposal?"

"I'm not sure," she said coyly. "You moved into the villa a week ago and have been sleeping in a room down the hall from mine and your daughter's ever since. Do you plan to keep on doing that?"

"Not if you'll let me sleep in yours."

"Then it's a yes."

He closed his eyes and let out a long, slow breath. "Thank you for that, angel," he said. "I've been a very sad and lonely man since my father died, disappointed in myself on many levels and so afraid I'd blown any chance I might have had with you."

"I've been sad, too, Niko," she said, "but it hasn't changed the way I feel about you. I love you. I always will."

"I love you, too, so much more than you'll ever know. I love our daughter and will protect you both for the rest of my life."

That night, they lay together in bed with Helen between them. After fussing all evening, she'd finally fallen asleep.

"How beautiful she is," Niko whispered, his gaze tracking her face feature by feature. "Her ears are like little shells and look how tiny her nose is."

"She has your dark hair," Emily told him.

"She has your mouth.'

She smiled. "She is *our* baby."

"Yes," he said. "And I think you should put her in the drawer so that we can practice making another just like her, *mana mou*."

They made love, taking slow delight in rediscovering each other. He traced his tongue over the pale blue veins in her swollen breasts. She kissed the scar on his shoulder where he'd been shot. With hands and mouths and whispered words of love, they found the magic they once thought they'd lost and made it new and wonderful again. And when, at last, he entered her, they clung together and let the passion roll over them in sweet, endless waves and carry them to the far shores of ecstasy.

Afterward, Emily curled up in his arms and, hearing Helen whimper in her sleep, murmured drowsily, "We really must buy her a proper crib, don't you think?"

"Tomorrow, my darling," he said, bringing his mouth to hers in a lingering good-night kiss.

He tasted of lemons and sunshine and all things Greek. Of the fabulous turquoise sea, the dazzling mango-tinted sunsets, the ethereal dawns.

He tasted of forever.

FREE

2 BOOKS AND A SURPRISE GIFT!

We would like to take this opportunity to thank you for reading this Mills & Boon® book by offering you the chance to take TWO more specially selected titles from the Modern™ series absolutely FREE! We're also making this offer to introduce you to the benefits of the Mills & Boon® Book Club™—

- ★ **FREE home delivery**
- ★ **FREE gifts and competitions**
- ★ **FREE monthly Newsletter**
- ★ **Books available before they're in the shops**
- ★ **Exclusive Mills & Boon Book Club offers**

Accepting these FREE books and gift places you under no obligation to buy; you may cancel at any time, even after receiving your free shipment. Simply complete your details below and return the entire page to the address below. You don't even need a stamp!

YES! Please send me 2 free Modern books and a surprise gift. I understand that unless you hear from me, I will receive 4 superb new titles every month for just £3.19 each, postage and packing free. I am under no obligation to purchase any books and may cancel my subscription at any time. The free books and gift will be mine to keep in any case.

P9ZEE

Ms/Mrs/Miss/Mr..Initials ....
BLOCK CAPITALS PLEASE

Surname ....

Address ....

....

....Postcode ....

Send this whole page to:
The Mills & Boon Book Club, FREEPOST CN81, Croydon, CR9 3WZ.